BLACK
FEET
DARK
HEARTS

BLACK
FEET
DARK
HEARTS

A Novel

WAGIH ABU-RISH

Cover Design by Riley Quinn

Published by Kirkland Publishing House in the United States.

Paperback ISBN: 979-8-9859152-7-3
Hardcover ISBN: 979-8-9859152-8-0
eBook ISBN: 979-8-9859152-9-7

First Edition

www.wagihaburish.com

To the over one million martyrs who died fighting for Algerian independence, from France.

When widespread physical rape was commonly practiced and later discovered, under French colonial rule of Algeria, one could barely imagine the depravity of the political, cultural, and economic rape that accompanied it.

Main Characters

SUHAIL SABER—Main character

KAMAL SABER—Suhail's father

MONA OWAIDA SABER—Suhail's mother

SUHAILA HASHIM—Suhail's first love in Amman

DR. HAMADAH—Suhail's professor in Amman

SALWA ZAHRAN—Suhail's love interest in Algeria

COMRADE—Suhail's resistance commander

MARCEL FIGARO—Corrupt winery owner

JULIETTE FIGARO—Marcel's wife

MAURICE—Juliette's father

GUY ANTOINE LA FONTAINE—Salwa's father

GILBERT SIMON—Private eye in Paris

GENERAL TOULOUSE—Powerful French General

JULIAN TOULOUSE—General Toulouse's son

JAMEELA—Elderly 'mother hen' supporter of the resistance

Contents

Chapter 1 1

Chapter 2 11

Chapter 3 23

Chapter 4 39

Chapter 5 55

Chapter 6 73

Chapter 7 85

Chapter 8 99

Chapter 9 109

Chapter 10 121

Chapter 11 135

Chapter 12 147

Chapter 13 159

Chapter 14 173

Chapter 15 185

Chapter 16 197

Chapter 17 211

Chapter 18 219

Chapter 19 231

Acknowledgements 247

About the Author..249

Chapter 1

Kuwait 1959

I was in my fifth secondary grade, one year before my high school graduation. Out of nowhere, a classmate of mine, Munther, nudged me in the chest and said, "Suhail, mind your business."

I looked at him with total surprise, as I did not know what he was talking about. I did not want to start a fight; I was just taken aback.

"Don't talk to her anymore," he added.

It took me a minute to figure out which girl he was talking about. She was like him, of Indonesian extraction, which was rare in Kuwait and of no definable ethnic status.

I told him I was not talking to her; I was talking to the student standing next to her.

"Don't give me this; you are an arrogant asshole; go back to your country, Palestine."

A Kuwaiti friend of mine intervened and told Munther that he was the asshole; that he was from Indonesia, a non-Arab country, and that I was from Palestine, a dear and persevering Arab country.

At that point, I could feel the societal and political stratifications surfacing. Where you came from mattered, and the issue of Palestine and its status seemed to surface all the time.

That small incident played a major part in firming up my thoughts to connect with my own roots. Gradually, I convinced myself that going to college in Kuwait or America, the two locations under consideration, may not have been the best choice. I decided to go to Amman to study civil engineering, just like my father specialized in. To me, it was an easy and natural decision. I liked physics and math, and I excelled in those subjects, which was opposite to how I performed in biology.

My father, Kamal Saber, had moved to Kuwait in 1952 and built a very successful engineering company, employing 190 civil, mechanical, and electrical engineers. When he first arrived in Kuwait, he shared a simple room with an engineering classmate of his. He used to wet a sheet to cover himself with, in order to sleep in 40-degree Celsius night weather.

Kuwait City was a small, sleepy town with mostly adobe homes. It even had a town gate, which was locked at night. He could not afford to eat at local restaurants for the first two years. What he dreaded most was *haboob*—the windstorms that carried fine sand, which penetrated most cracks and even settled in the nostrils of individuals.

Now, things are just the opposite, like comparing the abyss to the stars.

My mother was a housewife who was involved in the cultural and social scene. I did not care for it since her participation was shallow and it served more self-promotion than serious activities. It was my father who had attracted my interest and secured my respect. He was totally a self-made man. His grand-parents were illiterate, and his mother had finished only four years of elementary school while his father finished two years of high school. He had to peddle trinkets on the streets of Cairo to make ends meet, to support himself through Cairo univer-sity. Both he and his brother finished engineering school. My uncle finished his doctorate at the University of Illinois and was teaching mechanical engineering at Purdue University.

———————

My mother's claim to accomplishment centered on the fact she came from an 'Honorable' family. This was the designation given to families that claimed lineage to Prophet Mohammad. She always reminded me that I was an Honorable through her. I never cared for such designation, and it was, in my judgment, an oxymoron for Muslim Sunnis, since they always claimed that the prophet had good and bad relatives.

"How, then, could you be always 'Honorable,' being related to the prophet?" I used to ask myself.

What bothered me more than my Honorable status was the fact my mother was still calling me Susu at the age of seventeen. While Susu was a nickname for Suhail, it usually belonged to kids and not adults. My full name was Suhail Saber, and despite my repeated requests to be called Suhail, she insisted on calling me by my nickname, Susu!

My mother resisted my decision to study engineering at the University of Jordan. I had chosen this school because the majority of the student body was Palestinian, and I wanted to get to know those students.

My father, on the other hand, was methodical. He said he would look into the curriculum of the engineering school first, especially civil engineering, before giving me his opinion. His opinion came back most favorable. He advised that undergraduate engineering studies were no longer an exclusive specialty and that what the University of Jordan offered was more than adequate.

My mother was unhappy about my father supporting my decision to study in Amman. I could tell because she always wanted to brag in public that I was a graduate of America. Otherwise, my going to the University of Kuwait would have also suited her, by having me at home and giving her the chance to dote on me, like I was a ten-year-old kid.

My junior and senior years in high school were the most uncomfortable. Not only did my mother stick to her methods, but my father was also losing his patience with her. He started confronting her every time she would start a statement with, "We, the Honorables…"

One evening, when the temperature in Kuwait hit 45 degrees Celsius, he arrived home in a sour mood. He had to dismiss his employees early that day as the air conditioning units were not keeping up.

My mother opened the door for him, letting him know that she had fixed him his favorite chicken dish.

He snapped at her, "Who wants to eat hot food in this kind of weather? Don't you have the good sense to prepare an assortment of cheeses and cold watermelon?"

It was not the norm for my father to be so critical. He continued trying to tell her that it was the cooks who prepared our food and not her. He said, "You should have the wisdom to put better sense into the cooks for them not to cook when it is this hot."

My mother answered, "I know you are saying this to hurt my feelings; it is true that I did not cook with my own hands, but it is a chicken recipe known to people like us, the Honorables."

This is when my father lost it. "Honorables my foot; this title was bought for money from the Ottoman empire; there is not such a thing as being a relative of the prophet."

I was astounded at the turn of events and tone. My mother went into my parents' bedroom and started crying like a little baby, most unusual for a self-righteous person. For the first time, I thought my father had taken things too far.

But what does he mean about buying a title from the Ottoman empire? I wondered at the same time. I had never before heard of such an allegation.

Within ten minutes, I went to see my mother. I told her to blame the whole thing on the weather and that my father would come to his senses as his statements were said in anger, and that he did not mean what he said.

My soothing words did nothing, as my mother claimed that no one ever could insult the Owaida family in Palestine.

"If anyone dared, they would have had his head bashed," she added.

———

Things never went back to normal. My parents managed a superficial reconciliation, but their relationship seemed tense ever since that evening. Before, I was worried about which university to attend; now, I was concerned about something much more important: that my parents were not enjoying each other's company.

I picked up the phone and called my only sibling, my twenty-two-year-old sister, in Dubai. She was married to a Palestinian, a highly successful contractor, who asked for her hand after having been my father's client. My sister flew over the following week and took my mother's side all the way.

She criticized my father in the face and chided him by saying, "Just because you fight with Mother, you don't have to fabricate lies by claiming that my mother is not a true Honorable."

I don't think her visit made the slightest difference. I continued to observe that my father's attitude had changed. It became tepid, and he had shorter interactions with my mother.

It took three months for me to accept that there was nothing I could do to improve the situation. I continued to hope that time would correct things. In the back of my mind, I did not know if my father was right in attacking the so-called Honorables. I promised myself to find out, although I did not feel a sense of urgency.

———————

In a couple of months, I finished my junior year before heading to Amman to spend the summer in much cooler weather. It was our annual routine. My father used to fly over once a month, during the summer, and relax for a week at a time. As expected, he and my mother followed their routine by visiting family members and friends. On a visit to one of my maternal uncles, his sixteen-year-old daughter served us the usual Turkish coffee and sweets.

My mother leaned on me to let me know that my cousin had gotten prettier and more mature. She added, "If we let them know we are interested, she would wait for you till you finish your engineering."

That came from nowhere, as I felt I was way too young and saw my cousin as if she were my sister. I got really mad and said, "Maybe when you finish engineering."

That was not the last time Mother ever mentioned arranging my marriage. She was way off base, probably trying to busy herself with some new issue, since her activities with Dad had declined.

My senior year in Kuwait proceeded on an even keel. My parents' relationship continued with its new indifference. It seemed that both my parents resigned themselves to the new arrangement, without arguments or criticism of each other.

It was all right with me, although it did not feel ideal. My sister was busy with her first child and my mother filled in the time by visiting them once every two months. She made sure she visited while my sister's mother-in-law was not there.

The mother-in-law also came from a humble origin, just like my father did. My mother did not perceive her to be an equal, since she was not a university-graduate Honorable.

My concentration was on finishing my senior year and moving to Amman to study engineering. I did not need to study much as I not only could solve most problems, but I could derive each formula I used to work out the problem with. I could not finish the year soon enough.

I had many friends but only two close ones; they were both Kuwaitis. The three of us went into the desert and camped for three days. One of them drank Johny Walker Black Label scotch. My other friend and I had had two cold beers each day as we could not imagine drinking strong alcohol in 50-degree weather. The outing worked well, especially as both promised to visit me in Amman, and also agreed to stay with me at the eight-bedroom house.

As I was saying goodbye to several of my classmates, Munther—the Indonesian-born student who had confronted me the previous year—approached me and now apologized for his behavior.

It turned out that the girl in question was his sister. He told me she had gotten engaged in the meantime and was planning to move back to Indonesia to get married to her fiancé.

I congratulated him and we buried the hatchet, although there was not much to bury since we had never interacted since that incident.

———————————

I made sure I finished my more selective shopping in Kuwait City. There were many boutiques, mostly owned by Lebanese, which carried the most fashionable French and Italian designs. I bought two dozen items of each: trousers, shirts, shoes, and underwear.

My mother fastidiously separated my old clothing from the new and had them neatly packed. She and I were soon on our way to Amman to escape the oppressive heat.

Chapter 2

Amman 1960

I was anxiously waiting for the school year to start. I intended to take public transportation to school, but my mother would hear none of it. She insisted on buying me a large Peugeot. I wanted to buy a Fiat, far humbler than the Peugeot, and in line with the kinds of cars some students owned. My mother's argument was that the Fiat was too small for safety. I decided not to resist; I agreed to own and drive the larger and fancier car, though I secretly planned to park it away from class, so I would not seem to be showing off.

This is where I went wrong: parking was difficult to come by. There were no student garages or reserved parking spaces. It was 'first come, first served' for whatever could be used as a parking space. I should have visited the campus in advance, but only arrived half an hour early, thinking there would be ample time for me to park and make it to my classroom. There were no spaces, so I was ten minutes late, having parked half a kilometer away.

When I got to class, there were only three empty seats. I approached the first two to find out they were reserved with a stack of books each. The one I was trying to avoid was next to a student wearing a white headscarf. I was not religious and avoided females who wore scarves and males who grew stubby beards, supposedly signs of piety since this was what the prophet prescribed.

I sat next to her and looked straight, trying to avoid making eye contact with her. To my surprise, she looked at me and said, "He said nothing much. He just gave us the exam schedule. I will write it down and give it to you after class."

I kept trying to avoid looking her in the eye and said a faint, "Thank you."

At the end of the class, she opened a binder, pulled out a blank sheet, and wrote down the dates of the three tests and the final. She handed the sheet to me and left without looking at me much. I looked at her and observed that underneath the scarf was well-groomed soft hair and a clear facial complexion. She was pretty.

I went to two more classes; she was there. This is when I realized that, like me, she was probably studying civil engineering. I had no plans to connect with her, mainly because of her scarf.

───────────────

Two weeks into the first semester, my eighty-eight-year-old maternal grandfather died. I had to skip school for one day. He had been ailing for two years, suffering from lung cancer. He was a heavy smoker of cigarettes and water pipes.

My mother was inconsolable, although my grandfather had been in a coma for four months. Her response was to serve the most elaborate meal of mercy after the burial. Despite my advice to stick to three additional dinners, she insisted on accepting five. The tradition was that family and friends would sponsor additional meals in honor of the deceased family, to show their respect. It took one whole week before it was all over.

All through that week of mourning, I could barely study or even take proper notes. I did not know what to do at first. In the end, I swallowed my pride and approached none other than the girl with the scarf.

I sat next to her and immediately said, "I am sorry. I don't mean to be following you. It is just that my grandfather passed away last week, and I did not take proper notes in my classes. Is it possible for me to copy your notes? Do you mind?"

"No problem," she said. "I happen to work next to my home, at a print shop in the refugee camp. I will make copies of my notes and will give them to you tomorrow. Sorry, but I have no time today. I start work in half an hour."

Before this, I had never met anyone from a refugee camp. I did not know what to say. I was surprised that she seemed so comfortable with the fact she lived in the camp. She mentioned it as if it was another neighborhood.

When I got home, my mother told me she was expecting two couples to come by and extend their condolences.

I asked her if I could skip it to concentrate on catching up, since Father was also going to be there. My mother insisted, saying that I was then eighteen, an adult with all the responsi-bilities associated with such adulthood. I grudgingly accepted.

The following day, I tried to sit next to the girl with the scarf. There were no seats next to her. After class, she approached and gave me a stack of nine pages. I looked at the first page and I could tell there were a few words I could not read.

"Can we walk together to make sure I understand every-thing?" I asked.

She agreed.

"Before we start, I need to pay you," I said.

She said that there was no need, and that the owner of the print shop allowed her to make thirty copies a month, free of charge. I took a bundle of money from my pocket, not realizing the two hundred dinars I took out was more than her family made in one month.

She looked at the bundle and said, "I have to go. Go ahead and circle anything you don't understand, and I will explain tomorrow."

Her look at the bundle of money and her crisp takeoff to the bus stop made me realize I had been inconsiderate. My father always coached me to be humble and used to cite an example of the prophet's behavior. When the prophet ate rare fruit, he would bury the peel in the sand, so if the average man or woman saw it, he or she would not feel deprived.

My bundle of cash was much more than a fruit peel; it was a flaunting of wealth, no more and no less.

The following day, I planned and sat next to her. I told her that I was Suhail.

She looked at me and said, "Suhail!" and stopped for a while without saying her name.

I said, "It is okay if you don't want to share your name. I found nine words I could not read. Can you read these to me?"

She looked at me with a faint smile and said, "No, there is no problem; my name is Suhaila Hashim."

While I noticed the mention of her family name and its formal implication, I chose to overlook it. I took two quick breaths through my nose, smiling back. "I can't believe it! Suhaila!" I said, repeating her name, which was the feminine of my name.

I hesitated for a while but before I said anything else about our names, I pulled a stack of five hundred blank sheets from my bag and asked her to give them to the print shop owner in exchange for the nine copies she got from him, free of charge.

She got close to me and whispered in my ear, "I could tell from your clothes and from your money your parents must be very rich. Why can't you accept a small gift from a refugee like me?"

I was shocked at her statement, and I felt insulted. I said nothing. I put the stack of paper back into my bag and slowly left my seat, heading to the back of the class.

After class, I hurried to leave, passing next to Suhaila. When she saw me, she hollered, "Suhail, stop! Please stop."

I moved to the side to let the other students exit first. She looked at me after everyone had left except for our professor,

Dr. Hamadah. Suhaila looked at me straight on and said, "Pardon me. I was insensitive. It is all my mistake. If you want, we can spend ten more minutes to read to you the remaining words."

I felt too insulted to keep her company. I gave her the marked-up copies and asked her to write the words in question in a more legible way and to give them back to me the next day.

─────────────────

The following day, she gave me back the copies with all nine words rewritten and readable, without any challenges. I thanked her for her help and said nothing else. We both went our separate ways and sat several rows from each other. Looking at the board, I could see Dr. Hamadah looking at me. I figured he must have noticed my interactions with Suhaila.

A few weeks went by, with each of us avoiding the other, and with time, I consciously started ignoring her presence. That was until I could not see her anymore in any of the three classes we had in common.

The next day, I intentionally stood in front of the lecture hall and looked around to make sure she was not hiding from me. I waited for a minute after everyone came in; she still had not shown up. I got concerned. I thought that she may have fallen into hard times and dropped out.

At the end of class, Dr. Hamadah asked to see me.

"You have been looking for Suhaila Hashim," he said. "Am I right?"

I paused for a moment before I told him that I was. He then told me she was in hospital recovering from a bus accident. He explained that as she was being dropped off, her bag, wrapped around her shoulder, got stuck in the bus door. By the time the driver realized it, the bus had dragged her several meters. She was badly bruised but suffered no serious damage or breaks.

"I want her to be able to finish the semester," I told him. "I'm ready to share my notes with her, the same as she shared her notes when I was late for class."

He thanked me and said that he was planning to visit her in the hospital that same evening. I asked him if he could deliver copies of my notes from the three different courses, if I could get them done in time, and bring them back to him. He agreed.

That evening, Dr. Hamadah called me at home and told me when Suhaila asked who was providing the notes, he asked her to guess. She seemed to know who it was but decided not to reveal it. Dr. Hamadah told her that it was me, and only then did she admit she had figured out that much.

He also let me know she would be released from the hospital the next day. Without thinking, I went to my mother's favorite flower shop and ordered a fancy bouquet to be delivered to her that morning. I had to pay the flower shop extra to have the bouquet delivered within a couple of hours. When the bouquet was delivered, she knew right away that the bouquet was too expensive for her family members or friends to afford.

———————

To my surprise, Suhaila was in class the following day. She sat next to me. She was not wearing her headscarf. I found out later that the doctor had advised her to try to air out a couple of the serious scratches on her skull, though they were hidden by her hair.

As soon as she sat down, she had a broad smile on her face. "Are you crazy to send me such a gorgeous bouquet? I did not show it to my parents. They would have thought we were having an affair of sorts. I ended up giving it to one of the nurses."

"Let me know which one so I can be sure to start an affair with her instead," I joked.

Suhaila smiled, and for the first time I could see a real beauty, one usually muted by her headscarf. "Keep smiling," I said. "You look like a budding flower."

She lowered her head and said nothing, yet her cheeks blushed, radiant and rosy.

I wanted to hold her head and turn it toward me, to further gaze at her beauty, but I tapped her knee and whispered in her ears. "Look at me; look at me in the eyes and say nothing, just smile."

She obliged, and I again whispered in her ear, "I want you to look at me like this every morning and every day. You look heavenly."

"You are the one who makes me look heavenly," Suhaila said. "It all started with you. I don't want to think what will happen when it ends!"

I said nothing but asked her if we could have tea after class, and she accepted.

After class, I told her to follow me, but to pretend that she was not doing so. She followed me to my car. That further gave me away. When she saw the car, she hesitated before she got in. She immediately felt the leather seats and touched some of the knobs without moving them. When I saw the look on her face, I tried to mitigate the 'rich boy' situation by claiming it was my mother's car. My falsehood did not matter to her; to Suhaila, I was very rich, and she was poor.

I drove her to a coffee shop fifteen kilometers from the university. It was populated by a few connoisseurs. The coffee was twice as expensive as any other local shop. It used only Yemenite coffee, known to be the best in the Middle East and possibly the world. We both ordered coffee. She had never been to any coffee shop outside the refugee camp. She looked around to admire the fancy setup.

We sat on the floor, on top of a plush Persian carpet, with the coffeepot on top of charcoal briquettes. We had our backs against embroidered cushions, which were against a solid backboard. Suhaila looked all around and expressed how she was experiencing a rather pleasant, strange feeling, charmed by what she thought were unique surroundings.

I soon found out that the coffee shop's arrangement was more familiar to her than I thought. She told me that her living room was so similar, as they found it more economical to use a traditional setup than a more lavish, modern one. They spared the expense of buying chairs and tables. She was having difficulty relaxing. She said she had never been alone with a male, besides her brother.

I jokingly told her that if she felt dizzy as a result, just to hold on to me to stabilize herself. This is when she hit me on my arm and said, "You want me to get dizzy, don't you?"

"No, I don't want you to be dizzy for one second; I want you to be fully awake, and to look at me with these beautiful eyes. I want to visualize them clearly every night as I go to bed," I said.

We spent one hour together. It was like a dream. All what I wanted was for her to look at me and to look at her in return. I drove her to the bus station closest to the camp, where I dropped her off. She put on her headscarf all the way down before she got out of the car. I tried to give her my mother's sunglasses to cover her eyes, but she turned them down as they would have been more revealing, since they were so expensive and fashionable.

I drove back home to be met by my mother, who inquired about my getting home late. I told her that I was studying with a friend, and that I found him most helpful, prompting me to want to study together in the future. I wanted to see Suhaila every single day, if I could manage it.

———————————

Many of our classmates noticed our budding relationship. Most of them were deferential, as they avoided sitting next to me or her, making sure we could sit next to each other. This, however, was somewhat problematic, though I didn't realize it at the time. My original objective for enrolling at the University of Jordan was to connect with as many Palestinians as possible, but my infatuation with Suhaila completely eclipsed that goal.

I was gripped by my care for her. Not only did I feel I loved her, but I appreciated her calmness, honesty, and shining demeanor. I felt she was pure, and despite her challenging economic situation, she didn't yearn for the flashier aspects of life.

I wanted to test her devotion to humbleness. I bought her an expensive, cute handbag and told her I would keep it in the car for her to use when we got together.

She looked at me and said, "This is a very lovely bag, but I will not be using it. It does nothing for me. I want to be real by living within my means. I don't mind owning a bag like this if I could afford it routinely. Nothing is important to me except you."

I felt small, testing her. She sounded and looked so real and genuine. I was ashamed of myself.

"You're one hundred percent right," I said, and I apologized.

She told me she had not been sleeping well since she developed feelings for me.

"I am afraid that you and I do not have a future together. Not only will your parents oppose our relationship, my parents and brother will, too. They are kind people but will have doubts about us. You are a rich boy, and I am a poor girl; they will think that you will take advantage of me. I am sure our future does not look promising, and I am at a loss for what to do. I love you. I think I love you more than I love myself. I don't know how this happened so fast. We have been going out for one month and it feels like I have known you ten years."

"My mother tried to have me study in the United States, but I resisted and enrolled here, against her will," I said. "I think my mother will be the only one who may object to our relationship. My father is an angel. He will assess things before he gives his opinion. He usually decides wisely, as he came from a poor and humble origin. With the help of my father, I can defy my mother and in time, she usually accepts my decision."

She looked at me less than convinced and said, "*Inshallah,*" meaning, *God willing.*

And then she added, "My family also would feel there is a socioeconomic mismatch between us."

Chapter 3

Our relationship went so smoothly and so lovingly. None of our family members figured that our time together was not exclusively for study, but also for play. Separately, they accepted our version that each of us was studying at the library with other students. We used to find the most inconspicuous coffee shops for our rendezvous.

In time, we started touching and hugging, with thoughts and questions coming into my head. I was sure she was a virgin, but more importantly, I knew I was. I had no plans to have sex with her and she would not have let me. I never even seriously considered it. I was on cloud nine all the time. I maintained an A average, and she maintained a B average, at first.

She was more organized. She kept up with every detail our professors advised, and I helped her follow my lead. I told her that the surest way to master solving math and engineering problems was to first learn how a formula in question is derived. It took time at the beginning, but once she learned how to derive a certain formula, it saved time. In no time, she increased her grade average to B+ using my advice.

A month before the end of the first school year, I came down with a severe respiratory disease. My mother was so worried that she had our family physician make house calls every single day, for three days. Suhaila was beside herself and did not know what to do to contact me. She approached Dr. Hamadah and before she even asked him about me, he told her that I was sick and that he planned to visit me the following day.

It was unusual for professors to visit their sick students, but Dr. Hamadah used this to offer his tutoring services. The university allowed it, provided they never took a class with him afterward.

Dr. Hamadah showed up at the house, and most surprisingly, was accompanied by Suhaila. When my mother greeted them, she made sure she introduced herself as Mona Owaida Saber.

She was always keen on mentioning her maiden name.

I could hear Suhaila's voice and see her legs from where I was resting. Dr. Hamadah told my mother that Suhaila was there to share with me the notes from all three courses she and I were taking together. He added that he would have come alone to share his course notes, but he knew nothing about the other two courses. "This is why Suhaila is here," he explained.

My mother invited Dr. Hamadah into my room and asked Suhaila to wait in the living room. She forgot to ask Suhaila for the notes. In no time, Suhaila followed them and said "Hello," as she entered the room. She gave copies of the notes to my mother and left the room abruptly without excusing herself, and without saying goodbye to anyone. Suhaila's lack of proper decorum caught my mother's attention.

Suhaila must have felt uncomfortable having realized her awkward behavior. She was sitting in the living room, clearly mad at herself.

I later learned from Dr. Hamada that when he and my mother went to the living room, my mother was ready to probe into Suhaila's background, interested in her simple dress and headscarf. In typical Arab style, my mother looked at Suhaila and said, "What is your name, my love?"

"My name is Suhaila. I don't know your son well, but he had asked for my notes before, when he was late for class. Dr. Hamadah asked me to accompany him. He knows I took good notes."

"And where do you live?"

"I live in the camp next to the university," said Suhaila, "with my parents and my brother. We have ten relatives living at the camp. We originally came from Jaffa."

My mother took out five Jordanian dinars and tried to slip it into Suhaila's palm.

Suhaila pulled her palm back and said, "I am not here for money; I am here to share my notes with your son. I thought if I shared my notes with him, he would share his notes with me if I ever get sick."

"And do you expect him to visit you at the camp?"

"No, not really. Nobody visits us at the camp, except other camp residents. I am sure Dr. Hamadah will not mind delivering your son's notes to me in class. What is the name of your son?" Suhaila asked, pretending to be ignorant.

"His name is just like yours, Suhail," said my mother.

"Oh, my God, bless the names," Suhaila said. And then she looked at Dr. Hamadah, asking him if they could hurry back since she had to go to work.

My mother thought she had the upper hand. She came back into my bedroom after Dr. Hamadah and Suhaila left and said, "What is your relationship with that girl, Susu?"

"You mean Suhaila? Nothing. She is a fine girl and a good student. She always participates in class discussions," I said. I then added, "Well, she is good-looking and there are several guys trying to get close to her, but she is conservative; she keeps to herself."

"As long as you do not try to get close, do you hear me?" she said in a loud and threatening voice.

This is when I lost it. "I am not close to her, but I will get close if I change my mind, and there is nothing you can do about it. Stop treating me like a little kid and stop calling me Susu. I hate that name, and you don't seem to want to listen to me. I have told you a hundred times that I hate it, and you need to stop it. If you continue to use it, I will not answer you—do you hear me?" I said in a louder and more threatening voice, hoping to overtake her cynical tone.

It shook my mother up. She had to take a deep breath before she said, "You are imitating your father. You want to be like him, gruff and unsophisticated?"

"I know one thing for sure. I don't want to be like you. I want to be accomplished like him. He is a self-made man who had to sell trinkets in the street of Cairo to make ends meet. He sometimes ate fava beans for a week at a time because he could not afford any other kind of meal. He also loaned your brother money after he went bankrupt. So, tell me, is it better to be accomplished and self-reliant or Honorable and bankrupt?"

"You are growing to be evil, just like your father, using unkind and crude language," she said. At that point, I got up, put my clothes on, and started walking toward the front door.

Mother ran after me, "Susu, you are still sick; you will kill yourself. Come back, forget what I told you."

I did not stop and got out of the house. I drove toward the refugee camp. I parked half a mile away, as I did not want anyone to notice my car. As I got to the gate of the camp, a policeman stopped me.

"You live here?" he inquired suspiciously.

"No, I don't. I am here to pick up copies being made at the print shop; can you tell me where it is?"

The policeman showed me where to go.

When I entered the shop, Suhaila was there. She saw me and jumped in surprise, then immediately went into the bathroom. When the shop owner came over, I told him I had heard that he had very competitive prices, and that I wanted to make a thousand copies of a flyer and wanted to know how much it would cost.

Before he could give me an answer, Suhaila came out of the bathroom with her hand on her stomach. She proceeded into another room, seemingly to fetch her long coat, which she wore whenever she had a short dress on. She told the owner that she had a bad stomachache and needed to get home.

I gave the shop owner my phone number and asked him to call me with the price. I didn't think that he linked me to Suhaila or her contrived stomachache.

I ran out ahead of her and waited three straight blocks away from the entry to the camp. I wanted Suhaila to see me, but she kept looking at the ground, and didn't notice me until she was thirty meters away. I hurried toward my car, and she followed me.

When she got close to the car, she signaled to me to drive further out, which I did. Ten blocks from the camp, I saw another policeman. I parked next to him and told him that my car had suddenly stopped working. He said that he was directing traffic and could not help me.

I opened the hood and pretended to be fixing my car until I saw Suhaila, then I started the engine. She hopped in first and I drove on. "Don't say anything. Stay quiet. We will talk when we get to a place twenty kilometers from here," I said.

It was a land subdivision fixing to be put on sale, totally unattended. I drove my Peugeot uphill, on a dirt road, for over a kilometer.

I got out of the car, and she did the same. We went around the back and hugged each other in a most passionate and expressive way. I did not kiss her, nor did she kiss me. We just caressed and squeezed each other.

Minutes later, I held her face in my hands and said, "There is no one but no one who could ever separate us. We have belonged to each other from the first moment you laid your eyes on me, and I laid my eyes on you, and we will always belong to each other."

We sat on the ground, hugging each other. Suhaila looked at me and said, "You are the essence of my existence, yet how can I cause you to separate from your own flesh and blood, your own mother? I cannot do that. Our relationship, to continue, has to include your family and my family. We cannot be selfish and ruin the past to enjoy the future. The past will end up haunting us. I know. I am sure."

I told her not to worry and that I would try my very best to appease everyone, including my mother, but that I had to think of a practical way.

I was not fully recovered but went back to school anyway. I did not want to be away from Suhaila. Dr. Hamadah asked me and Suhaila to stay after class.

He looked at us and smiled. "I know what you are going through, and I empathize with you. Love is not easily suppressed. Yet, love has many enemies, even among those who had fallen in love once and forgotten about it. Let me know if and when you need my help. I will try my best to help you. I was once in your shoes and her family ruined it for us, as she was promised to her cousin, all for a parcel of land. This is why I have never married. You need to be careful not to lose the battle in more than one way; you may lose your family, and one or both of you may abandon the love you have for each other."

It was double-edged advice, one about hopeful love and another about heartbreak. I looked at Hamadah and said, "I will never abandon Suhaila, and I know she will never abandon me. She is like the air I breathe. I cannot do without air."

She looked at Dr. Hamadah and said, "Neither could I. I know that my life will become meaningless without Suhail."

Dr. Hamadah wished us good luck and again reminded us he was there for us.

————————

When I went back home, my mother was anxiously waiting for me. I told her, in a calm voice, that it was best for the two of us to wait a few days before discussing the subject of Suhaila.

She looked at me as if I did not know what I was talking about. "I don't want you to get stuck in the mud of what you think of as love. She is not in love with you; she is in love with your money."

"If this is what you think, then I will make sure that Suhaila will get not a single penny of my father's money," I said. I emphasized my father's money, for I knew that my mother's family was just about broke when my parents got married. They accepted my dad's humble origin, since he was willing to save them from downgrading to a lower standard of living.

————————

The first school year was over successfully for both Suhaila and me. We needed to figure out a way to get together without alerting her brother, who was very protective of her. My most secure way was to order copies at the print shop, where Suhaila worked for three hours a day. Little did I know that my mother asked her driver to follow me and report his findings.

In no time, she was aware of my plans, including those that involved getting together with Suhaila for an hour after work. It even got easier for my mother: her chauffeur bribed the print shop owner, and it was no challenge for him to call my mother daily and report to her all about our plans.

Two weeks later, my mother visited the refugee camp while Suhaila and I were spending time together. Mother had already visited Suhaila's brother, Ahmad. She'd told him about my relations with Suhaila and while assuring him that the relationship was 'innocent' thus far, she was concerned that we might be carried away in the future. She tried to give Ahmad twenty Jordanian dinars, but he turned it down.

When Suhaila got home, Ahmad was ready and prepared for the occasion. He told her outright that she was tarnishing the honor of the family and that nobody would believe that it was a genuine love story, but a situation where she would be perceived as a money grabber. He offered not to disclose her relationship to their parents if she promised to end it. It was a long and piercing reprimand.

Ahmad was a high school Arabic language teacher and knew how to present the subject and make a humiliating and effective presentation. While an older brother acted as a surrogate father, especially when the father was incapacitated, Ahmad knew well how to make Suhaila feel guilty. Above all, he made her feel guilty about their father's potential reaction.

Suhaila's father had a heart condition and Suhaila loved him and her mother, and did not want to put any pressure on her sick father. She teared up and took a few minutes before she could answer Ahmad. After she collected her thoughts and composed herself, she asked Ahmad if she could end the relationship in one week, to 'say goodbye to Suhail and apologize to his mother'. Ahmad accepted, on the condition that she would not see me more than two times before she broke it off with me.

Suhaila called and told me about what had transpired but said nothing about what she planned to do after the breakup.

She visited my mother first. Mother was expecting her as Ahmad had informed the print shop owner, and the owner had informed Mother. Mother was all ears and acted graciously. Suhaila told her she wanted to talk to her first in order to be ready for Suhail's heartbreak and for Mother to take care of him after the break.

Mother told Suhaila not to worry, and that she was most appreciative of her help. Before Suhaila was about to leave, Mother looked her in the eye and said, "I want you to promise two things; the first is to resist all attempts by Suhail for the two of you to stay together, and the second for you to seek to be truly happy by associating with your own kind. We are members of the Honorables. We don't marry just anyone. We marry from the outside, but they need to have redeeming attributes; excuse me to say, but I don't think you and your family have any such attributes."

Suhaila started crying quietly and asked to be excused.

I was going up the stairs when I found her sitting down, crying.

"Suhaila," I said and tried to hug her.

She pushed me back and said, "Don't touch me. Go sit in your mother's lap. She knows what is right and what is wrong. She knows that neither I nor my family have the attributes to have anything to do with you." She got up and ran down the stairs.

I ran into our flat looking for my mother. She was in the kitchen instructing our cook what to prepare. There was a bowl of green beans on the kitchen counter. I took the bowl and threw the beans all over the kitchen floor, something I had never done before. I wanted Mother to know how mad I was.

I looked at her and asked, "What did you do to Suhaila? Is it the same thing all over again? That you are Honorable, and she is dirt poor? Did you tell her that she did not possess any classy attributes? I bet you made her feel worthless. Yes, you enjoy insulting people. Fuck all the 'Honorables' and fuck their mothers and fuck their ancestry. I feel sorry for my father and now I feel sorry for myself, but I will not quit. I will be with Suhaila and if I cannot be with her, I will not want to be in your life!"

I could tell from her looks that my mother was shocked at the level of my anger.

I ran down the stairs and drove to the camp. I went directly to the print shop. The owner held me back from going inside to look for Suhaila. I had seen her leave the front to hide in the back as soon as I got there. Another employee must have called the police at the gate of the camp. He was at the shop within five minutes.

The policeman said, "Sir, you look like a gentleman, but if you do not leave right away, I'll have to handcuff you and take you to the police station."

I agreed to leave, but before leaving, I told the print shop owner that I would be coming back to leave a letter for Suhaila. He said that he would deliver it to her as long as I did not insist on seeing her.

The following day, I dropped off a letter. In it, I told her I could not live without her and that she and I could leave Jordan, get married, and live in Lebanon. I ended the letter by asking her to leave me a note that she had received my letter, and afterward, if I did not receive an answer, it would mean that she did not want to see me anymore.

I kept going back to the print shop to see if she had received my letter. I received a note from her on the third day, which confirmed in her handwriting that she had received it and that she would not be responding to it for two weeks, but possibly later.

A month later the print shop owner handed me a letter from her, in which she told me how tortured she was being separated from me, but that after factoring in her family's opposition and her father's frail condition, she was unable to make a clear decision. Instead, she decided to extend our separation for one year, after which she would decide if her feelings for me had survived.

At first, I was furious and at loss for what to do. After realizing that my choices were impossible due to her father's failing health, I sent her a note back telling her I was willing to wait, and that I was sure that our love for each other could not be extinguished in one or even ten years.

It was an aimless and trying time after that. I went to Aqaba for two weeks where I swam intermittently for eight hours every single day until I got exhausted and crashed until the following morning. By the time I got back, my father was there for his routine week in Amman.

As soon as he returned, he took me into his bedroom, which he did not share with my mother, and said, "Your mother told me her version of the story. I don't believe her. She embellishes things to suit her interest. You don't need to tell me anything. Just be careful and do the right thing."

I was resigned to the fact that I needed to wait for a year before Suhaila followed her heart and came back to me. I was antsy and frustrated. I could not concentrate on anything.

One day, the radio described two major incidents regarding the Algerian revolution, one in France and another in Algeria. They both involved the explosion of military facilities, blown up by the Algerian resistance fighters. At first, the two reported incidents did not have any special impact on me, but as I kept hearing more about the fierce fighting taking place in Algeria and realizing that I would not hear from Suhaila for a year, a thought crossed my mind.

Why not volunteer to fight with the Algerians? After all, they were valiant Arab nationalist fighters who needed all the help they could get, and I was aimless and mad as hell.

I clipped several articles about the Algerian war of independence and shared them with several friends.

Two friends expressed similar feelings to mine. They both said that they would have volunteered if their circumstances were different. It so happened that both had family responsibilities.

I told myself that I had no responsibilities whatsoever, and that Suhaila was the only one I wanted to take care of. Their sentiments influenced me considerably. I went back to the two and probed further. I determined their expressions were genuine.

I still was not sure and sought more solid assurances and direction. I went and talked to Dr. Hamadah. He turned out to be the ideal person to talk to. After I explained to him that Suhaila was planning to give me an answer in a year, I expressed my desire to volunteer and fight with the Algerians. He was more than supportive of my idea. He said that the Algerian fighters were the most courageous Arab fighters that existed since the eighth century, and that they were even more valiant than the forces fighting under Saladin in the twelfth century. Dr. Hamadah volunteered to help me travel to Algeria. I was shocked at his enthusiasm for my idea.

Within three weeks, he handed me a complete file outlining who to contact and how to proceed. It was most surprising to me that he could do all that in a short period of time.

I soon found out why. He was the head person in Jordan collecting donations to support the Algerian liberation effort against the French.

Little by little, he started revealing detailed information about his support for the Algerians, which included facilitating the road for volunteers like me. At one point, he stopped mincing words and gave clear and direct advice. His plan was for me to go to Egypt first, to connect with a specific and not so secretive committee, all made of Algerian revolutionaries.

Chapter 4

August 1961

My father returned to Kuwait. I kept to my room, despite my mother trying to placate me in her own condescending manner. I refused to join her for meals and kept eating cheese and cold cut sandwiches in my bedroom. I used my seclusion to quietly pack my clothes. Fortunately for me, I had several visas on my passport, including one for Egypt. My father had always insisted we secure as many multiple entry visas as possible, including those to Lebanon, Egypt, Kuwait, France, Spain, and the U.K.

Five days later, I wrote a note to my mother and put it in my safe. It was the safe I'd kept my savings in. I kept peeping through my bedroom door until I could sneak out of the house without being noticed by my mother or the cook, and when the driver was on an errand.

When I got to the airport, I hid in a corner until it was ten minutes from boarding. Then, I called my mother and told her I left her a letter in my safe, and I gave her its combination without the last two digits. I told her to try her luck from zero to ninety-nine and that she could open the safe. I wanted her to waste time so she would not be able to reach me before flying out.

I knew what my objectives were. I wanted to hurt my mother but above all, I wanted to prove to Suhaila that I was not the pampered rich boy, and she was not a lesser person, an undeserving product of a refugee camp.

I wanted her to see that I did not only care for the far-away fighters of Arab Algeria; I also had great feelings and empathy for my own downtrodden Palestinian refugees, with Suhaila being one of them. It was something she and I never discussed. I genuinely sympathized with her situation, giving herself one year to think about our relationship, continuing to live in a refugee camp. One year, I thought, was long enough for her to take my adventure and its implications into consideration.

In the letter, I told my mother that I was leaving Jordan and that I would be back in touch soon to let her know where I was heading. I made it clear that she was the cause of my departure. My letter was simple and without any sentiment.

When she managed to open the safe and read the letter, she must have fallen on her knees and started crying, just like she had done in similar situations. Yet, she always composed herself, and in this case, probably searched for my savings. I took all twelve thousand dinars, enough to sustain me for three years in Jordan. I was told later that she waited for the driver to return, to take her to the refugee camp as she wanted to confirm her suspicions that Suhaila accompanied me.

———————

Strangely enough, even after my departure, my contacts were maintained with the print shop owner. He was eager to share with me all the news about Suhaila. He liked the fact that I treated him with so much importance and went to the trouble and expense to call him from wherever I was. He asked me about my daily activities, and I described what I could in detail.

He told me what happened after my mother found I was gone: she barged into the print shop, looking straight at Suhaila. Suhaila was surprised but indignant. My mother took a deep breath and said, "Where is he?"

Suhaila said nothing at first but then said, "Who are you talking about...Suhail?"

"Yes, Suhail, who else?" said my mother.

"I have not seen Suhail in three weeks, and I have absolutely no idea where he is. Maybe he is with one of his friends, or maybe he went to Aqaba."

"No, no, he did not go to Aqaba. He left the country; he left without you. This is good."

Suhaila looked at my mother and said, "Good or bad, he never asked me to go with him and I would not have gone if he had asked me."

My mother looked at Suhaila and said nothing yet exhibited an expression of *who are you to turn down my son?*

Suhaila, thinking I was hiding somewhere in Jordan, went to see Dr. Hamadah. Hamadah minimized his role, although he was corresponding with the committee in Cairo.

He told Suhaila that I had visited him two days earlier and informed him I was leaving Jordan, but did not say where I was going. He added he didn't take me seriously and asked if I had really left Jordan. Suhaila told Hamadah that her news came from my mother, who was convinced I had actually left town.

When Hamadah asked Suhaila what she planned to do if it was true, she said that my being in Jordan or outside Jordan had no bearings on her plan, and that she was intent on waiting for one year before making up her mind. As of that moment, however, she said that she could not conceive of living without me.

Hamadah asked her to let him know if she heard from me. She asked Hamadah to do the same, but he said that he did not expect to hear from me at all, although we had agreed that I would let him know as soon as I left Egypt.

———————

In Cairo, there were two pleasant surprises. First, my Jordanian savings could have sustained me in Egypt for six years, as the cost of living there was much less expensive. The second surprise was how welcoming my Algerian hosts were. It was almost embarrassing. They showed unusual respect for the Palestinian struggle, but in a practical manner, they appreciated a volunteer like me, who spoke fluent English and decent French. Their cadre spoke Arabic and French and were hard-pressed for English-speaking helpers to connect with sympathetic Europeans.

Of the six males I interfaced with, I could understand five of them well, since they intentionally spoke in classical Arabic. The sixth, Hadi, could understand me, but I could not understand him. He spoke with a purely Algerian dialect.

When I told one of them that I could not understand Hadi, he said that I would in two weeks. I didn't know what he meant. He said that I needed to speak in the Algerian dialect, otherwise I could easily be identified, and that I would need another month of dialect training in Algeria before they would let me interface with the common man. It was disappointing, as I thought Arabic spoken with an Algerian dialect was not Arabic at all.

Before long, I was introduced to an Egyptian, Omar, who had already been dealing with Algeria for a good five years. He was smuggling weapons from Egypt. He was a graduate of Al-Azhar University and was, as with Al-Azhar graduates, an expert in the Arabic language and its structure.

He was the one who told me that the North African Arabs spoke most of the same words I spoke, except that they used shorter, Amazigh vowels, which made the same word sound significantly different. After all, the Amazigh people and their language existed a thousand years before the Arab invasion of North Africa.

Once I differentiated between the words with Arab vowels and the same words with Amazigh vowels, I could then tell the difference and start to speak the same words in both dialects. I surely was very skeptical, but in two weeks I could understand half the words and some sentences. Little by little, my language training progressed, and the Algerian dialect grew partially discernable.

The time came to plan my trip. I was supposed to be smuggled through Libya to get into the southern part of Algeria. But they said that going from the south to the north of Algeria posed a great danger, as much of the desert was made of French military districts. When I inquired why they chose a route known to be dangerous, they said that the better routes were too costly. When I asked how costly it was, they said around three hundred dollars.

I said nothing for a while, as I had around thirty thousand dollars in my possession. After I realized how tight-budgeted the pro-Algerian revolution efforts were, I said that I could secure five hundred dollars.

One of the group members said, "You can? Then we can easily get you over through Almería."

When I asked about Almería, he said it was in Spain, with over ten percent of the population being Algerian.

In three weeks, my Algerian pronunciation got even better, but I struggled to speak full sentences in the Algerian dialect. They told me I would spend three weeks in Almería where, after intensive conversations with my hosts, I should be able to pass for an Algerian.

I thanked my luck that even though I was somewhat fair-skinned, I was brown enough, just like my father, to pass as an Algerian. My mother was almost blond, through her Bosnian roots, on her mother's side.

———————

The following week, I flew to Madrid, where I followed their instructions to the letter. They provided me with the names of three hotels, but I wouldn't know which they'd booked for me until I met with my contact at the airport.

An airport cleaning lady approached and slipped a note in my hand, which had the name of the designated hotel. When I got to the twelve-room inn, the room was clean, but the bed reminded me of what a night security man would use at a typical construction site in Kuwait, making beds out of discarded lumber to sleep on during the day.

In the morning, there was a knock on the door. It was another cleaning lady. She slipped another note in my hand. It was in Arabic that said that there was a blue Fiat waiting for me in front of the hotel.

The driver of the car nodded his head and directed me to get in. He said nothing but shook my hand. Within fifteen minutes, he dropped me off after directing me to get into another car. Again, the new driver shook my hand and said nothing for twenty minutes. Then, he turned to look at me sitting in the back seat, and gave me a full smile.

"Welcome to Spain."

It took eight hours to get to Almería. The atmosphere there was completely different. I was taken to a neighborhood that looked and sounded more Algerian than Spanish. Everyone spoke Algerian Arabic. The music in the streets was completely Algerian.

The moment I got out of the car, my companion said that from now on my name would be Zine and to forget that Suhail existed. He gave me a new fake ID and a sheet of paper, which included a full new background, with the name of my supposed father, mother and five siblings, not to mention the names of an elementary and a secondary school in Constantine city in Algeria. He told me I was lucky I knew some French. He asked that I pay attention to my hosts, especially when they used French words in their conversations, and asked that I try to insert the same words when I spoke Algerian Arabic.

When I went in, I was met by a middle-aged couple. The woman was wearing a traditional Algerian flowery dress. She started speaking to me and addressing me as Zine. She introduced herself as Zahra and her husband as Mohammad. The first thing she said was that my clothes were too fancy to be an Algerian from Almería.

She asked me if I could buy different clothes in the morning. I suggested to her that if she could wash some of my shirts and slacks but not iron them after, we might do with no new clothes.

She thought it was a good idea and said, "Then we do not have to guess as to the size of clothes you may need. But before I do this and make you look less attractive, let me call my daughter to look at you."

I thought to myself that even in serious matters, looks come into the picture. I was pleased when her daughter, Wallada, was just twelve years old, and not some sort of romantic hopeful. Zahra only wanted to expose Wallada to the looks of a rich Palestinian, though she was careful to tell Wallada that I was originally from Constantine but was working in London, trying to conceal my relationship to Jordan and the Palestinians.

Wallada was a refreshing addition to my stay. She asked about London, and I practiced talking about it as if it were truly part of my background. We played volleyball together and teased each other the whole time. Our interaction helped a lot in my becoming more fluent pronouncing the Algerian dialect.

———————

In the morning, I was taken to another house, where I was taught to use a handgun. After practicing for a couple of hours, I was deemed trained. Three weeks after my arrival in Almería, the time had come to head to Algeria.

I was taken to a small motorboat. There I met two young females; they were in their early twenties. They shook hands with me and then showed me their special IDs. One was called Amina, and her ID showed that she was twenty-two, and the other, Fatima, was twenty-four. They showed their IDs because they were supposed to be my sisters, and all three IDs showed the last name of Bouahmad.

We planned to use the boat to go to Oran, around 210 kilometers away. We were instructed to use the motorboat for 190 kilometers, after which we would drop the motor in the sea and row the last twenty kilometers.

They gave us nine loaves of bread, sheep's cheese, and enough water to last twenty-four hours. They also gave us gloves and a Vaseline-like substance, to use if our hands suffered blisters while rowing. Amina and Fatima were talking all the time to each other but pretended that they were also talking to me.

I was given two contact names in Oran with a background sheet for each, in case I became separated from the two girls.

The trip took eight hours, without incident, and I was happy to arrive in Algeria.

Although they showed some interest in my background and possibly in me, personally, Amina and Fatima followed their instructions and disappeared as we hit the shore. I followed two men to a donkey-driven cart, where they made me lie down with my two large *mantas*—rough blankets bundled to contain my clothes—and then emptied thousands of cucumbers on top of me, filling up the cart to the brim.

In no time, they removed the cucumbers and poked me in the side to rise. I looked around to find a casbah-like neighborhood. I could hear Algerian Arabic being spoken. I was guided into a house with a large front room. Six women stood there, looking at me. One was at least seventy, the other five in their early twenties.

I said hello in Middle Eastern Arabic, which caused the five young women to burst out laughing.

One of them, fair with green eyes, said, "Hola," and moved around swiftly, "You are another cucumber man. Welcome. I am Salwa," she said.

Evidently, others before me had been transported in the same cart.

The older lady ushered me toward her and pulled off my shirt without asking me, and I did not know why. I was topless at that point. I presumed she wanted to make sure I was not hurt on the way over there. Salwa and the other four laughed.

One of the four, who was introduced as Nabila, addressed Salwa and tried to conceal what she was saying by speaking fast.

"It looks like your eyes are on him. By God, he looks hand-some."

"Not my eyes, it is your eyes that are fixated on him; look at his underwear, it is prettier than mine—he's not my kind of man," said Salwa. When I heard what she said, I immediately pulled my slacks to cover my partially exposed underwear.

Four of them laughed, but not Salwa. She started talking in French to them, asking them not to say anything anymore as I could understand Algerian Arabic. One of the four told Salwa that she could tell that Salwa was interested in me, and that she even noticed the quality of my underwear.

The older lady pulled me into what served as a bathroom. There was a slab of marble on top of a two-foot high chair. She sat me on it and tried to take my slacks and underwear off.

This is when I said in a very loud voice, "No."

"Why no? Don't be shy. You smell of cucumbers, from your head to your toes. I am eighty years old," she said.

I could hear laughing outside, and then I heard Salwa saying to them, "No, this is not right. Would you allow an eighty-year-old man to give you a bath?" she asked in an accusatory tone.

In the end, the old lady and I compromised, and she ended up giving me a bath in my underwear. I now know how she saw me: as if I were one of her grandchildren.

Half an hour later, I went out into the front room. I was all clean and without the smell of cucumbers, wearing my only set of fresh clothes. To my surprise, Salwa and the other four were waiting for me. It was only seven in the morning, but it felt like it was evening since we were on the boat all night, without sleep. They had prepared a spread of boiled eggs, cheese, toma-toes, and French bread.

I told them that although we had cheese and bread on the boat, I had not eaten any. I felt cold, as well.

"Do you have any hot food, like soup or stew?" I asked.

Salwa hurried into the kitchen and returned with a pot full of chicken couscous. It was left over from the prior day, Friday, the day Algerians invariably ate couscous.

I looked at it and nodded. Salwa went into the kitchen to heat it. She came back in five minutes with a glass of hot tea with mint. I thought she could read my mind since I always drank tea with mint.

By the time I got my second cup of tea, the couscous was ready, and it was delicious. I ate it with gusto, then looked at Salwa and thanked her for the delicious food.

She said that she did nothing except warm up the food and that it was the old lady, Jameela, who fixed the couscous.

Salwa then asked one of the four, Samia, to show me where I could take a nap if I were sleepy.

I was, and I told Salwa so.

Samia looked at Salwa and said, "Come now, I know you'd like to show him where to sleep."

Salwa looked at Samia sideways, then ushered me to follow her. I did. She took the cover off the bed and asked me to lie down, which I also did, and she then covered me.

Four hours later, I woke up to find all the girls and Jameela having lunch. I sat in the corner before Salwa said that I should engage in the conversation since I needed to further practice talking with an Algerian dialect.

Everyone used a spoon, not a fork and a knife. It was like Suhaila had described what she and her family used. My face fell.

Salwa looked at me and said, "What is wrong with you? You look sad. Why?"

I said that I was not. To change the subject, I told them they could ask any questions they had about Jordan and Kuwait.

Another of the girls, Najwa, started. "Describe your house in Jordan."

I did not expect them to ask about me, but about Jordan and Kuwait as countries. When I tried to describe Kuwait, Najwa insisted I describe my house in Jordan. I decided instead to assume Suhaila's setting. I lied and gave them the description of Suhaila's house, with two bedrooms and one bathroom. I also talked about my family, also by describing Suhaila's family instead, claiming that I had one brother.

I was about to tell them that my brother was sleeping in our cousin's bedroom, just like Suhaila's brother did, when I realized the same could not apply to me. He was doing so since Suhaila turned twelve and because she was a female. I stopped myself and told them that my brother and I slept in the same room, next to our parents' bedroom.

Salwa was the one who asked no questions; she listened intently to my answers.

At the end, she said, "There is something wrong here. I don't believe everything you said. I am the one responsible for intelligence gathering in this group. Your answers contain too many details. This is unusual unless you are making up things or assuming the character of someone else."

I had to answer Salwa, and said, "Yes, I am assuming my brother's personality, except he does not like to give as many details as I do."

Salwa did not press the issue, and we moved to go through the typical items in a refugee camp. I pretended to be talking about such items, just like a camp resident would have done routinely. It was a great idea, as it prepared me to engage in casual conversations. We spent an hour at a time, taking a break every fifteen minutes.

When it was time for dinner, I insisted on helping. I fixed a fine-cut cucumber and tomato salad with a lemon and oil dressing. My paternal grandmother allowed me to help her whenever I used to visit her, before she died.

That evening, I ate a lot and told everyone that I would wait at least four hours to go to bed. Salwa said she would wait with me and asked the others to wait if they could. They all wanted to go to bed early since we were starting at five in the morning. I started to think that cute Salwa might have a crush on me.

When we were alone, I was surprised to hear that she was not happy about my answers regarding my personal life.

She said that she planned to have everyone tell me about their situation and expected me to correct anything I may have embellished about my own.

When I asked her what the big deal was, she said that it was important and that to work as a team we had to know each other well to make up for each other's weaknesses.

I went silent and said nothing. I looked around the room to avoid looking at Salwa. I was expecting Salwa to express a hint of her feelings toward me, and at that point I intended to tell her about Suhaila. I got a glimpse of Najwa spying on us, standing behind the curtain of the door. I realized Najwa was jealous of Salwa and must have been disappointed not having caught the two of us in a compromising situation. Najwa left when she realized I saw her.

I did not think Salwa saw Najwa, but five minutes later, Salwa said, "I also saw Najwa. I was expecting this from her, and I am going to bed."

I could not tell then if Salwa held back from expressing her emotions for her own reasons or because she expected Najwa to spy on her.

I spent the four days after my arrival venturing out with two of the girls at a time, to acquaint myself with the city, listen to the common man speaking, and study his behavior. I noticed so many new things. It was a great experience. After each outing, I would sit down with all five girls and attempt to describe and answer questions about my outings. After six weeks in Cairo, Almería, and Oran, all five agreed I was ready for the first job.

Chapter 5

I sensed the depth of hate that the average Algerian harbored against the French occupiers. During their 130-year occupation, they brutally relegated Algerians to the point of becoming non-persons. To France, Algeria was never an entity on its own, but part of France, which effectively designated Algerians as intruders in their own land.

The average Algerian knew where this stance emanated from and what it meant. It meant that the average Algerian was worth nothing and was treated accordingly. They were distant, third-tier persons, ranking below the French settlers and the Spanish and Italian imports. The imports were used as buffers between the French and the Algerians and were guided into becoming participants in the oppression of the native population.

Dependent on the French for their daily living and unable to act openly, the Algerians had to devise surreptitious acts to be effective. The first undertaking I engaged in involved stealing a machine gun. The French conscripted some Algerians into their ranks. Salwa had already chosen the target: there were two Algerian soldiers guarding the villa of a major French winery owner. They were stationed in front of the villa, while two other French soldiers guarded the back. The Algerian soldiers were approachable; the French soldiers were not.

Salwa explained the plan. I was supposed to act as a sophisticated young Algerian businessman, properly dressed, followed by two girls. I would ask for help from one of the two Algerian soldiers, while a third girl distracted the other. One of the two girls with me would use a handgun to threaten the soldier I was seeking help from, followed by my easing his machine gun out of his hands and putting it in a special bag. Then we would hop into a waiting car and speed away.

I told Salwa that the plan had one major flaw, even if every other step worked. "What about the other Algerian soldier and his machine gun? He could easily strafe us before we get to the car!"

Salwa said I was right, but the whole plan depended on two additional factors. The first pertained to the position of the two French soldiers, which would be relayed to us by the villa cook hanging a black shirt on the line if it was a no-go, and a white one if it was okay.

Secondly, it depended on the cook's ability to empty the magazine of the second soldier's gun, as both the cook and the soldier slept in the same room. "The danger may come if, after the cook empties the magazine, the second soldier replenishes it," said Salwa. "In this case, we have no choice but to have the cook kill the second soldier and flee with us," she added.

I said nothing after that because I knew Salwa was on top of things, and she knew I had taken notice of her thoughtful plan.

When I asked why risk so much for one machine gun, Salwa said that the French were too spread out and usually chose to overlook anything that didn't include death or major damage.

———————————

To say I was not nervous would have been a lie. That evening, I wrote contact information so that my father, mother, and Suhaila would be informed if I were to die or be captured. I gave the list to Salwa and said, "In the case of Suhaila, please include a red rose."

After surmising that I had a girlfriend, fiancée, or even a wife, she said, "I will give this to Jameela, but no, she will not send any flowers; there will be no need."

I didn't know whether she was trying to cheer me up or herself.

We woke up at five in the morning, and by 6:15 we were all ready—I with a goatee and the girls with wigs, among other makeup items. We were at the villa by seven. Salwa saw the white shirt hanging.

The whole plan was nearly scuttled when a barefoot Algerian pushing a vegetable cart hit Salwa. She fell a few meters from the first Algerian soldier. Though Salwa was bruised on the face, she quickly signaled to everyone that there was no harm and that the fall was helpful.

The soldiers saw the incident, and she took the opportunity to approach one of them to ostensibly seek help for her bruised cheek. He laid his machine gun on the ground to help her. The rest became easier than brandishing a handgun. I followed my instructions: I picked up the machine gun, and we all ran to the waiting car—an old taxicab with fake license plates.

I didn't know how the two soldiers analyzed our heist; all I knew was that the second Algerian soldier tried to strafe the taxicab, only to find his magazine was empty.

We didn't go to the house right away but were dropped at another safe house. We waited until 2 a.m. to return, wanting to ensure we weren't identified. When we got there, Nabila met us with open arms. She took Salwa aside and asked several questions. One I overheard was about me.

Nabila asked, "Did Zine know the whole plan?"

Salwa answered that I didn't, and that I wasn't told that the entire operation had been tailored to test me. I interpreted this to mean that the whole thing was a fake holdup.

I went toward Nabila and Salwa and said, "Obviously, you harbored suspicions about my commitment. That's why you set up this fake operation. I think you should forget about me, as I feel you don't trust me."

"No, no, you're mistaken. It has nothing to do with trusting you. It's just that we have you scheduled to engage in some serious future tasks—tasks that you should be most qualified to undertake. We didn't want to unnecessarily endanger your life, so we took additional precautions we didn't tell you about."

"What precautions?" I snapped.

Salwa then took me into another room and said there were two snipers—one facing the Algerian guards and another facing the French guards—just in case things didn't go smoothly. When I told her I didn't believe her and that the whole thing was make believe, Salwa held my face, gave me a peck on my lips, and whispered, "Believe me; otherwise, I wouldn't have kissed you."

I didn't know how to react. The kiss certainly changed the nature of my concentration. I had only revealed to Salwa a day ago that I was in love with Suhaila. Yet, she ignored all that and exposed her emotions to me. It didn't make sense unless she intended to steal me from Suhaila.

Thoughts raced through my head. I had gone to Algeria to impress Suhaila and convince her not to leave me, and now I was being lured by one of the people who were indirectly supposed to help me convince Suhaila. I knew then that my love for Suhaila was much too strong to be abandoned in less than two months. I said nothing and planned to give no hint of my interest or lack thereof. I didn't want to insult Salwa by openly rejecting her.

I left Salwa behind and went back to the living room, pondering what to do next. My intention was to let Salwa know that Suhaila was my one and only love. Not knowing how or when to do it, I decided to go to bed as an escape measure. After all, it was after 2 a.m. When I woke up at ten in the morning, I pretended nothing had taken place. We had the day off, and the plan was to go to the souk and browse around. Nabila and Najwa went together. Salwa insisted she had things to do. I thought she was also wondering since I hadn't reciprocated her romantic move.

I was the one who said, "I'm sure Salwa would have accompanied us if she weren't busy."

It was one more non-indicative statement.

In the evening, I lay in my bed thinking about what to do. I told myself there were two extreme measures: one was to return to Jordan, and another was to stay and respond favorably to Salwa's advances. My thoughts were crystal clear; both were totally unacceptable. This is when I told myself that I would stay in Algeria and stick to my mission, but to do that, I had to find a way to relay to Salwa that, due to my continued love for Suhaila, she was not the object of my romantic affections.

I decided that Jameela, the eighty-year-old lady, would be the best conduit to relay my decision to Salwa. I asked Jameela if she could give me a back massage since I was suffering from some back stiffness. She was more than happy to oblige.

The bathroom was clean but spartan. I sat on a wooden stool in the middle of a large brick-paved floor. There were three pots of water around the stool. Jameela dipped a small glass into the first pot, which contained soapy water, and after pouring the liquid on my head, she used the other two pots to rinse the glass and wash the soap off me.

In the bathroom, I told her everything.

She told me to tread very carefully since Salwa's mother had committed suicide six months earlier. When I told Jameela that suicide was not allowed in Islam and rare among Arabs, she said that if I knew the circumstances, I would understand, and that both Salwa and her mother were Amazigh, members of the ethnic group that inhabited North Africa before the Arab invasion.

The news about Salwa being Amazigh was a revelation to me. Also, Jameela's news about Salwa's mother convinced me to do nothing for now, and instead to proceed only if I could surmise that there would be no slight to Salwa as a result of my rejection.

Najwa tried to approach me in the meantime. I took the opportunity to directly but deferentially turn her advances down in the presence of Salwa. I was also trying to send an indirect message to Salwa as I told Najwa that I had someone I planned to marry in Amman. It was meant to relay, particularly to Salwa, that it had nothing to do with her looks or personality; rather, it had to do entirely with the fact that I was already committed.

I recalled Zahra giving me a book about the Amazigh. I went to my room to read it and learn as much as possible about the Amazigh tribes.

I had just finished reading about the Roman Invasion of North Africa and the Romans' abusive treatment of the Amazigh people when I heard a ruckus. Salwa was arguing with a man, which meant that it was someone from the outside, as I was the only male in the house. When the shouting got louder, I went out of my room to check on things.

The man, Naji, introduced himself and seemed to know who I was. He excused himself right away, and as he was leaving, he gave Salwa a stern look and said, "There is no other choice. You need to carry out the plan and you need to explain it to Zine."

Salwa looked at me, exasperated, and said, "Don't worry about it. It's a small thing. We will take care of it."

When I asked for an explanation, Salwa proceeded to her room. I went back to my room and resumed reading, but with every intention of finding out in short order since my name was prominently mentioned.

At dinner, I tried to address the subject with a gentle approach. I said that I didn't need to know right away, but someone should explain to me how I was involved in what Naji was discussing. Nobody said anything. Salwa left the table before she finished her dinner.

———————————

After dinner, Salwa knocked on my door. I let her into my room, and she sat in a chair facing me.

"I think I owe you an apology. I have lied to you in the past and now I plan to tell you the truth. To be honest, under the circumstances, I had no choice. I lied to you when I told you that the operation at the house of the wineries' owner, Marcel Figaro, was real. It was not. It was all made up to boost your confidence in yourself."

I looked at Salwa with complete disgust and said, "To boost my confidence, possible, but how would a fake operation help me learn how to fight the French?"

Salwa looked at me and said, "I agree with you. I was just following orders. You are not going to be fighting. You will infiltrate the French settlers' social scene."

I laughed and said that the whole thing must have been a joke. Salwa said that it was not a joke at all. She tried to explain that since her comrades learned that I was carrying around thirty thousand dollars, a considerable sum against the cheap French Franc, they decided that my best use was to utilize the money to infiltrate the settlers' high society, befriending Marcel Figaro. She added that the cook, the cleaning lady, and the two

Algerian soldiers were all helping the Algerian National Libera-tion Front—FLN—just as she and I were. Those four were supposed to get me close to Figaro.

I paused for a long while and then said, "Now I understand. The kiss was to support the cover, wasn't it?"

"It was, partially, but it was also a genuine show of attrac-tion," she said.

I said that her actions were unusual; it was rare for a woman to approach a man so quickly in Algeria.

She explained that while my thinking was right, it did not exactly apply to her, for her father was French and that she had spent half of her life in Paris. I could see the French in her.

I said nothing more about her approach and went back to the serious business of my new role. I told her I didn't travel to Algeria to play detective, and that I had to consent before I would engage again.

She looked at me almost meekly and said, "I will relay what you told me and will give you their answer. Again, I am sorry."

———

The answers from Salwa's superiors came through two days later. They asked me to reconsider, since what they were pro-posing was most beneficial to the revolution. They emphasized that they had not used such techniques in the past, but that they found in me the ideal person to extract precious information from Figaro. In their opinion, it was such important infor-mation that, if retrieved, it would be worth more than twenty successful battles against the French. It was not the answer I was expecting. I felt that if I were to turn down their plan, I would be abandoning them. I told Salwa I needed to think about it more. Their argument and the fact that I had not spent enough time to become a seasoned fighter convinced me to say yes in the end.

When I relayed my acceptance to them, I did so in writing, in a sealed envelope. I insisted that befriending Figaro would be the one and only espionage activity I would involve myself in and that I would need to deal with someone else other than Salwa.

I got back their answer agreeing to the first condition but asked me to deal with Salwa as she was the only one that spoke classical Arabic, French, and English. Figaro also spoke all three languages, as he had lived in Aden for eight years, being cared for by his English maternal grandparents. I didn't know if I made the right choice. I told Salwa that I had asked for a different contact person than her, but under the circumstances, I would deal with her. When she heard that I had asked to deal with someone else, she gave me a pensive and sad look.

For the following two weeks, Salwa acted as my tutor, trying to improve my French. I have to admit that she was an excellent teacher. She became very formal with me, and I with her. My French improved considerably. She told me that Figaro was a womanizer, although he was married to a gorgeous twenty-one-year-old, whose father was also a winery owner who had fallen upon hard times. Figaro had salvaged his father-in-law's three wineries.

Salwa wanted to review some love and sex terms with me. She was thinking of Figaro's love life and the probability that such terms would eventually surface. She said that I could skip this part if I felt uncomfortable. She clarified it was nothing personal on her part.

I told her to go ahead. She spent one day exclusively on love and sex terms. She then declared that her tutoring was over, and the following day she would share with me the details of the start of the plan.

I looked her in the eyes and said, "Don't you think confining yourself to the first part of the plan would not give me the whole picture? Knowing the whole plan from the start makes it so much easier for me, and would help me answer any questions, especially by suspicious parties."

"I agree with you, but the decision is not up to me. I will let you know later."

In three days, approval was given, and she explained everything. She told me that the FLN had no experience with espionage of this kind.

She poked her finger into my chest and looked into my eyes endearingly, and said, "Who do you think we are? We are simple and honest people who want to live in dignity. The society you talk about and the foods you describe are things we have not experienced, nor do we have a feel for. You, on the other hand, can act naturally and extract information without the other side suspecting anything. You will work in an environment you are familiar with. We know how to physically and technically spy on the French, but we are not socially sophisticated enough to mingle with the upper crust of the settler society. There are Algerians who do, but they are all lackeys and stooges, not operatives like you."

"Your role was determined from the start," she said. "I was chosen because I had lived in France for over ten years."

She then explained that Figaro was a self-absorbed and show-offish thirty-year-old man, with a net worth of over five million dollars. She asked me to read about Aden, where Figaro lived for over ten years, and learned to speak Arabic but never learned how to read it. He also spoke fluent English and decent Italian. I explained to Salwa that I mostly mastered my English through socializing with my American schoolmates in Kuwait, mostly children of oilfield workers.

Salwa handed me a new detailed background sheet. It said that I could keep the name Zine Bouahmad, and that I was born in Constantine but moved to Jordan with my family at the age of ten, where I'd lived until I decided to come back to Algeria to learn the winery business, with the aim of starting one or more wineries in Jordan.

My late father was Abdullah, and my mother Farha. I was most impressed with the fine details and above all with the ability of such contrived details to be corroborated. I went over my new background a hundred times until I could recount them in my sleep. Salwa and the other girls quizzed me for two hours, and I passed with flying colors.

Salwa made herself scarce when there was nothing to do or rehearse. The next meeting was devoted to my introduction to Figaro. I was to accidentally run into Mustafa, the cook, at the vegetable market where he was supposed to be buying carrots. I was to ask him if he knew of any place to buy maroon carrots. He would then lead me to a vegetable stand that sold the maroon carrots and then would invite me over to prepare a Syrian/Palestinian dish of stuffed maroon carrots in tamarind sauce. Mustafa would serve Figaro the maroon carrots and if he liked that dish, Mustafa would ask me to meet with Figaro. If Figaro did not like them, we would continue with another dish.

Everything went according to plan: my running into Mustafa, all the way to Figaro sampling the stuffed maroon carrots. Figaro thought the stuffed maroon carrots were delicious and, on his own, asked to meet me.

By then, I had moved into an upscale neighborhood and fashionable apartment where I lived on my own. It was all easy as when I counted my U.S. money, it was still slightly over thirty thousand dollars. That allowed me to afford the luxuries of Oran, with unlimited purchasing power.

Mustafa relayed to me what Figaro had said.

"Your friend is very interesting, and I could use some of his special ideas and recipes to surprise my friends. After all, we, the French, are best known for our avant-garde and sophisticated social life."

I told Mustafa to let Figaro know I was not available that week, but I would be in two weeks.

To my surprise, Figaro met me with his wife, Juliette. She also was half-English and half-French. Above all, she was stunning.

Even I had to admit she was more beautiful than either Salwa or Suhaila.

Figaro was quick to break the ice. "Please, call me Marcel and call her Juliette. I have plans for you. I can see that you have picked up some French mannerisms. I hope you can share with me some of your special recipes; I am excited to share them with my friends. I mean, I intend to share the food, not the recipes themselves."

Throughout dinner, Figaro was most admiring of Juliette. He repeatedly kissed her hand and her cheek. He never kissed her on the lips. Both thought the stuffed maroon carrots were a 'grand' dish. Each of them asked me a few questions, with no hint of suspicion. Juliette asked more than Marcel, and she showed much sympathy and admiration for me.

As I was leaving, I thanked Marcel and Juliette most appreciatively and told them I wanted to invite them to my apartment the following month. They both agreed cordially. I shook hands with Marcel and kissed Juliette on the cheek. Before I pulled away, she grabbed my buttock. I was very surprised and had to take her hand off before Marcel could see us.

She looked at me sideways with her beguiling eyes and said, "Don't worry, I know what I am doing. I just couldn't resist. Au revoir."

I went back to my apartment and, the following day, met with the girls. I told them what had transpired, but kept Juliette's daring advance to myself until I could meet Salwa alone. Then I told her exactly what had transpired with Juliette.

She was not surprised; she told me she thought something of the sort might take place. And then she said, "You are lucky. The thing I was thinking of was different."

When I asked her what she had expected, she told me that she was afraid Marcel would be the one to hit on me.

When I gave her an inquisitive look, she said, "Marcel is a sex fiend and bisexual. His attraction alternates between the genders on a regular basis."

This is when I firmly grabbed Salwa's arm, "Listen, Salwa. I want to help the Algerian revolution more than anything, but I will not go to the limits you are hinting at. I will go back to Jordan tomorrow morning."

She looked at me and said, "I totally understand. I don't want you to accommodate Juliette and surely not Marcel, but I will leave it up to you to handle it any way you feel comfortable, as long as you don't compromise our efforts and contacts. You need to keep in mind that Mustafa's life is in your hands. It is true that he and Marcel are lovers, but if Marcel finds out that he is associated with us, he will not hesitate to hand him over to the army in a split second."

"What did you just say? Mustafa and Marcel are lovers?"

"Yes, they are, but it is not what you think. They were lovers before we recruited Mustafa, and we did not know about it till later. We are also in a bind. If we drop Mustafa, we might trigger something in him where he may inadvertently reveal himself. He is a simple cook; he is not politically sophisticated."

I grabbed Salwa's other arm tightly. "Did you ever sit down and think of how many things I now know that were supposed to be revealed to me before I started spying for you? Do you?"

She looked at me with confusion and said, "You are hurting me; do you hate me this much? I did not plan any of it." Her flushed face made me realize I was overreacting.

I let go of her arm and told her I really liked her, despite the confusion and challenges they were exposing me to. She apologized and said that revolutions were always challenging and messy, and that they had to deal with limited finances, limited forces, and limited and awkward logistics. "Nobody is intentionally trying to trick you or harm you, least of all me," she said. She then grabbed me by the back of my neck and gave me a kiss on the mouth.

I told her to stop it and not to try to do this every time we got into an argument about our course of action.

"You can't do this to serve the revolution. It would be the same if I were to sleep with Marcel for the sake of our struggle," I said.

"No, no, I am not doing this for any other purpose than the fact I find you very masculine and attractive, not to mention sophisticated, although you are two years younger than me."

I looked at her with piercing eyes, for it was the first time she was telling the truth.

I sarcastically asked her what I was supposed to do with Suhaila. "Is she this easily dispensable?"

Salwa said that she was not, and that all I needed to do was to take a vacation. When I asked laughingly what kind of vacation she was talking about, she said that it was a vacation from thinking about Suhaila and instead responding to her advances.

This is when I asked, "Are you sure you are not more French than Algerian? You speak like a young French woman," and proceeded to my room.

That night, I locked my door for the first time. I was concerned about my own level of resistance. I thought Salwa would enter my room, and the next thing I would do was to grab her and make passionate love to her. My concerns were well-founded; I could hear someone in the night trying to turn the handle of the door. Whoever that was, he or she tried three times and stopped. I briefly thought of opening the door but did not.

In the morning, I felt good for not opening the door. I went into a pensive period with little interaction with Salwa or any of the other girls. Jameela was the first to notice. She approached me and said that she knew what was going on and that I had made the right choice.

I spent two weeks with the girls and did not engage with any of them till the last day, before I went back to my fancy apartment.

Salwa sat with me, and we discussed what to expect next. She wanted to know if our disjointed exchanges had altered my plans. I assured her they had not.

Chapter 6

A week later, I had Marcel and Juliette over for dinner. I fixed them the Palestinian national dish, one with chicken and the other with lamb, one with cauliflower and the other with eggplant. I told them that the dish was called 'upside down', but it should be called the 'mother of paella' since it was supposed to be the origin of the paella dish. They enjoyed our cultural exchanges. Marcel was properly cultured. He had studied the French, British, and Yemenite cultures well and he added much to the conversation.

Juliette was mature for her age but was less interested in cultural nuances. Nevertheless, she had an egalitarian outlook on life, and she opposed the French colonial practices in Algeria. Not so Marcel. He supported France's claim that Algeria was part of France, but I could sense that he was doing so to protect his commercial interest, and that if he were truly free of personal interest, he may have taken a stance similar to Juliette's.

I did not spare any expense that evening. I had engaged the services of a principal server who sometimes worked as a sommelier at a top-rated restaurant in Oran. I served a premium

Algerian wine, from a winery which originally used imported old vines from the Bordeaux region. Marcel and Juliette were most impressed, and Marcel confessed that my choice was better than anything he had in his cellar. He did not know that I used Salwa's connections to secure a library wine from one of the premier winegrowers, through the services of a Frenchman sympathetic to the cause of the Algerian revolution. The same person also provided me with a sixty-year-old VSOP cognac.

Marcel and Juliette were most impressed with my spread. They loved the food, the wine, and cognac.

It seemed that Marcel, while quite young, had a prostate problem. He went to the bathroom three times during dinner.

The second time was right after we finished drinking wine and before we started with the cognac. It was then that Juliette put her right hand on my crotch, which was another shock to my system. I had not anticipated that she would go that far, but considering what Salwa had informed me about Marcel, I realized on the spot that I should have expected side play on Juliette's part—but why me? She was one year my senior and a stunning beauty.

When I tried to take her hand off of my crotch, she said, "Don't worry, Marcel has a dozen teenage girlfriends."

I did not want to get confused or get into something detrimental to my purpose in knowing the Figaros. Furthermore, my commitment to Suhaila was intact. My thoughts were fast but fleeting. *I had one challenge, dealing with Salwa, but now I have a similar but much more dangerous one, with Juliette.*

After we finished our cognac, Marcel returned to the bathroom. Juliette massaged my crotch with a firmer application.

While I did enjoy being sought after by such beauty, I wanted to be firm in resisting.

On their way out, Juliette said that she could not think of a better meal that wasn't French, and that she wanted to prepare it for her cooking club members. She asked me if I could come to her house sometime to teach her the recipe.

To be polite, I answered, "I will if you teach me how to cook Algerian couscous and Algerian tagine."

Both those recipes were used in the Middle East but originally came from North Africa.

I really put my foot in my mouth, for it sounded like I was responding to her advances and more.

After that dinner, I went to see the girls. I told them it went much better than my best expectations. Salwa and I went out for a cup of coffee, at my request, where I told her about Juliette's sexual advances. She said that she had not expected Juliet to be that forward, that soon. She added that she needed to check with higher ups to figure out what they needed me to do.

"No; I don't need any help in figuring out what to do. I have no plans of maintaining any relations with anyone other than my relations with Suhaila—end of story."

Although I was also sending a message to Salwa, I felt she liked my statement; she must not have wanted to have a potential competitor. She seemed to want to take her own exclusive chances of developing a relationship with me.

She said that she could not advise me for two reasons. The first related to the fact it was a decision above her grade and the second related to the fact that any decision on her part may appear to be self-serving.

Again, I told her that the final decision was mine and mine alone.

This is when Salwa said, "I am not particularly talking about this matter, but you need to realize that serving the revolution, within acceptable perimeters, is the utmost important task. Otherwise, you would not have left your life of luxury and came here to Algeria, wanting to carry arms."

"Carry arms? Where are the arms? It looks like I am carrying my own penis, or at least others want to carry it for me. You know how strange it feels to be a sex object in order to eventually become a freedom fighter? What shall I tell Suhaila when I go back? 'I had great sex in Algeria, all to impress you!' Do you hear how ironic and convoluted the whole thing is?"

She looked at me with a confused expression. "I know. Don't you know that I know, and that I feel what you feel? I wish it were different. Do you think I enjoy involving you like this? It disturbs me but let us not talk about it. What is done is done. Let us change the subject."

———————————

Before I got an answer from Salwa's boss, I was surprised to get a knock on my apartment door. It was 8 p.m. and there was Juliette. I did not expect that the surprises would keep coming, and I was slow in figuring things out. I told Juliette that I was not expecting her and that she should have let me know, so I could prepare a program of sorts.

Juliette took me by the hand, seated me on the couch, and sat next to me. She looked me in the eye, moved my hair off my face to the side and said, "I know that you are worried about Marcel finding out. Let me assure you he does not care. He thinks he is Casanova, but he is not anywhere near him; he overdoes it, and he ends up not satisfying me or his other partners. Furthermore, I do not like to make love to one who makes love to men, especially when he makes love to Mustafa."

I pulled back, and pretended that I did not know and said, "Oh my God, Marcel is bisexual, and he sleeps with Mustafa? How about Mustafa? Is he bisexual too?"

"No, he is one hundred percent homosexual. That is why Marcel hired him in the first place."

"No, this can't be. I have serious reservations about socializing with Marcel. People will think I am homosexual too."

I thought this subject gave me an opportunity to probe into Marcel's activities. "This is too serious and unacceptable to me. I will not deal with Marcel until I know more about him. He seems to take too many risks and endangers his friends and acquaintances. What else is he involved in? Drugs, smuggling, what?" I asked, trying to get Juliette to open up.

"No, no, Marcel does not violate the law; he is also not a violent man. Sex is his thing. I take this back; sometimes he violates the law, but no one is prosecuted for that. Sometimes he goes to the Qabil districts, all the way to the Mostaganem region and picks up young girls and makes love to them."

"You mean Qabil prostitutes," I said, trying to play ignorant.

"No, they just kidnap them off the street and make love to them and then they let them go, after they deflower them," Juliette said.

"You mean they rape them?"

"Yes, Marcel and his friends pick up fifteen- and sixteen-year-old girls and rape them. It is a common practice among the French, Spanish, and Italians to pick up girls and women across all ages. The authorities prosecute no one."

I wanted to continue, but did not want Juliette to notice my keen interest in everything relating to Marcel. I was disturbed by the new revelation and halted the romantic advance Juliette had started.

I told Juliette that I needed to calm down after all this news and for the two of us to get together the following week, after I had cooled off. Juliette was understanding. She ran her hand over my face and then gave me four or five kisses. I gave her a small peck on her mouth and asked her to call me first to let me know when she wanted to get together.

———————

Salwa's boss responded three days following Juliette's surprise visit. He claimed my descriptions of casual sexual encounters were commonplace in France and Europe yet were completely inappropriate for genuine revolutionary groups. My return to Jordan was decided upon; the plan had to be harmless to the revolution.

At the women's house, I asked to speak with Salwa in private. When we were in a secure room, I told her about Marcel's activities in the Qabil districts. Salwa asked me if I was sure, and I told her that Juliette had described the activities. Four or five Jeeps would take men into a Qabil village, and upon spotting a young, beautiful girl, a couple of Jeeps would drive past her while the other men would confront her. They then would kid-nap her and take her to an empty orchard, where she would be held down so Marcel could rape her.

Salwa looked at me and nodded as if it were a scene with which she was familiar. Still, her eyes filled with tears; she began crying softly and then left my room. I followed her and asked her gently if she cared to explain to me why she was crying. At first, she tried not to give me an answer. Then she asked if she could meet me alone at my apartment the following day. I said yes, yet I did harbor some concerns that she was going to approach me romantically again.

When she came over, she was just like Juliette, held my hand and sat me down on the couch. She looked into my eyes intently and took a deep sigh.

"The reason I cried is because what you described about Marcel is exactly what happened to my mother. My father picked her up from the village street and raped her. When I got to be eight, he found me and kidnapped me. He sent me to France to live with his mother until I was eighteen."

She took another deep breath. "Although I was only eight years old, my mother had told me about how my father raped her. Over the years, I became friends with my paternal grand-mother. She became conflicted, showing her care and love on one hand, and trying to go by my father's warning, never to allow me to go back to my mother. At eighteen, I ventured and told my grandmother that I was a product of rape by my father. She was most understanding. She even cussed at my father and described him as derelict in his duties. After she told me she believed me, she sent me back to my mother.

"My mother was always in agony, and she never got over her rape because she could not discuss it with anyone in the village. They all would have thought she was loose and got pregnant by a villager. Recently, after I finished university and got a job offer, she sat me down and told me she was no longer concerned I could not support myself, and that I could manage without her. The following day, she committed suicide. As a result, I promised if I ever get the chance, I will kill my father in a split second."

Salwa burst into tears. I hugged her to make sure she would not collapse on the floor, but I also teared up. It was my greatest shock since arriving in Algeria.

I collected myself and whispered in her ear, "You should feel no guilt and you're honoring her by doing what you're doing now. Hopefully, I can help."

It took Salwa minutes to calm down and longer to resume our quiet conversation. She said that she could not share more details with me then, but she would try some other time. I told her that there was not much time and that we were wasting so much time between meetings, and that I needed to decide, partially based on the details of her mother's story and many others like her.

She could not talk for a while. I took her to my guest bedroom, where she lay in bed. In half an hour, she woke up and looked somewhat refreshed.

She sat next to me on the couch and said, "I know you want to be a brother to me. This is not the time or the place for such a discussion. I will tell you some details this afternoon and will tell you more in the future. This is a long story; it has been going on as long as Algeria has been colonized by the French. It has just sped up in the last seven or eight years. But the French are not the only culprits; they allow the southern Italians and the Spanish to do the same. Some of the French rapists give the victims to their Spanish and Italian workers after they deflower the virgins. Sometimes, the French rapists kill the girl if they find out that she was not a virgin."

Salwa continued and asked me if Marcel had shared the victim with his workers. I told her I did not know, because I decided not to continue with the conversation and risk arousing Juliette's suspicion. I then stopped Salwa and said, "I want to know more, more from you and more from Juliette."

I asked her to tell her superior not to end my efforts for the time being, as I wanted to know more about Marcel's crimes. I told her I wanted to use the subject of rape as an entrée into Marcel's political activity, since I thought he knew much that would be beneficial to the revolution.

We agreed to meet again the following day for Salwa to educate me about the history and nature of rapes in Algeria.

"You mean the rapes by the Pied-Noir?" she asked.

"What is the Pied-Noir?"

She told me it meant Black Feet, and it was what the French and other European settlers were called. When I asked why, she said that there were different explanations, but the best one was that when the French settlers started importing southern Italian and Spanish low-wage workers, they arrived bare-footed and with the exposure of their feet to the sun, their feet darkened and ended up being called Black Feet. She added that later, the label applied to all settlers, including the French.

The following day, we met and discussed other aspects of a suspected total of 200,000 rapes that had taken place throughout the occupation of Algeria. They started much later than the inception of the occupation, in 1830. No one properly chronicled the start of the rapes or their progression. They never stopped once they started, and they were still ongoing.

There was some suspicion that the rapes had decreased in the past year, as the settlers were worried more about their survival than about their sexual pleasures.

The settlers preferred the Qabil girls over most Arab girls. Perhaps they found them more attractive. Hardly any of the crimes had been reported. The figure of 200,000 was a bare minimum, arrived at by French activist political scientists.

When I asked Salwa if the young girls resorted to any kind of protection or hiding, she told me they did, according to her mother. The young girls initially started applying henna to cover their private parts. This caused the rapes to decrease for a time, but they eventually returned to the prior level.

Then the young girls, with the help of their families, started tattooing their breasts and their genitalia, but once again, the decrease in rapes was only temporary. Salwa said that her mother had already tattooed herself before she was raped.

Finally, some girls resorted to smearing their bodies with sheep manure. That was the most effective, but it still didn't bring a complete stop

I could barely believe what I was hearing. It was a story out of another realm. As Salwa enlightened me, I grew angrier and angrier at Marcel. I told Salwa that I was insistent not to quit and that possibly my mission had become more important than carrying a gun and fighting.

At that point, she grabbed my head and kissed me on my forehead, a kiss of respect. I emphasized to her that if her superiors did not accept my continued efforts, that I would do it on my own, and for her to relay my sentiments with great intensity. She promised she would and said that this time she would campaign on my behalf since she also felt so strongly about this issue. I then slipped my cupped hands to the back of her neck and kissed her on her lips. She was surprised but said nothing initially, pausing before she said, "Thank you."

Four days later, she called me and came over to my apartment to let me know her superiors turned down the idea first but, after she advocated in a heated series of arguments for my continuing with my efforts, they relented.

This is when I wrapped my arms around her waist and gave her another kiss on her lips. She was pleasantly surprised at my move. I kept it at that and told her to keep matters up to me. I knew how to handle things. I did not want to go into the details of the limits I would go to. In my mind, I was willing to do many things I had not contemplated doing in the past, before I learned about the rapes.

Chapter 7

Soon after, Juliette invited me to dinner. She emphasized that Mustafa had not been involved in the food preparation; it was her doing.

When I arrived at the house, she was wearing a long, silky, off-white dress.

I immediately asked about Marcel.

"He is gone with Mustafa to another gay friend's house. I suspect they're having a threesome affair."

My naivete surfaced when I asked her why people did such a thing. Again, I wanted to use my disgust to prevent a sexual affair with Juliette, but it did not work. She said that she did not know, and that she did not care, and that Marcel always respected all her wishes, including her extramarital wishes.

Juliette said that food needed another hour to bake and that we should not wait idly. She took me by the hand and led me into her bedroom.

"This is my bedroom," she said. "Marcel and I sleep in separate rooms."

"Why?"

"This way we each have privacy and can engage with other partners freely."

"Yours is not much of a marriage and not even a real relationship; it is an arrangement," I told her.

She then reminded that it was much more normal in France to have such arrangements than most other countries.

She added, "The arrangement could be a real marriage, or it could be a mere arrangement, short of a real marriage. Part of the arrangement is to agree on what to call it. Marcel and I call it a marriage."

I was very nervous, much less about betraying Suhaila and more because I was still a virgin and did not know how to properly proceed. My experiences of sex had been merely kissing and playing with females' breasts.

Juliette came to the rescue. She told me not to worry and to relax, for she intended to take the lead. I was elated and relieved to hear her say that. She took off her silky dress and got completely naked. She then took off my shirt and my T-shirt. She pushed me on my back onto the bed and started giving me a massage from my neck down. Before long, she unbuttoned my belt and took off my slacks and briefs.

For the first time, I was exposed to the additional sex acts of massaging and blowjobs. She was slow, deliberate, and most methodical, not to mention most considerate. She knew how not to over-arouse me. After fifteen minutes of careful acts, she guided my hands and mouth, seeking my participation. I responded to her guidance and in a short time, we were having full intercourse. It ended up being most satisfying for both of us.

We indulged in a great and varied French meal, consumed a bottle of premium French wine, and followed that by drinking port. Juliette then took me to her room, by my arm again, and we had another course of very intimate sex. I was most pleased as I was exposed to soft and elegant sex acts, acts which I had no idea even existed. I rationalized that what Juliette managed to teach me in one evening was something that enhanced my prowess, to be applied when I would have sex with Suhaila.

Juliette gave me a juicy kiss before I went back to my apartment.

Shortly after I arrived back home, there was an unexpected knock on my door. It was Salwa, who clearly understood the surprise on my face. She didn't even say good evening; she just looked at me. I think both of us wondered if I owed her a description of what had taken place earlier.

I pulled her into the apartment and sat her down. I wanted to exhibit some affection, but Juliette had consumed it all.

I think Salwa realized that much. After she collected her thoughts, she asked, "How was it?"

Saying nothing and with an inquisitive face, I pretended not to know what she was talking about.

"You don't have to say anything," she said. "I should not have asked such a question. Was the evening successful, in your opinion?"

I didn't know what to say, so I was intentionally vague. "It was a good start. It all depends on what happens next."

When Salwa asked if I was planning my rendezvous with Ju-liette as a routine, I told her that I was, as long as Juliette was providing me with important information.

She then asked what kind of information I secured that even-ing. I was prepared in advance as I did not want to appear I was only there for sex. I told her that I believed Marcel was partici-pating with other bisexual partners to commit his rapes. This was my assumption based on what Juliette had told me.

Salwa nodded and said nothing, but her attitude toward me cooled off, and I imagined it was because she was thinking about my sexual time with Juliette. It confused me. I did not know what to do. If I were to establish a relationship with Salwa, things would get much more tangled than they were after just merely making love to Juliette.

———————

The following week, Juliette called again and invited me to another dinner. I had to confess I was anxious to go. She was a great and compassionate sex partner. She taught me a lot in one evening, and I was hoping she would teach me even more.

I assumed that again I was invited because Marcel would be engaged in other activities. It seemed that since Juliette enjoyed her sex with me a lot, she got impatient for more and gambled by inviting me without knowing Marcel's exact schedule.

The day came. As she orchestrated our engagement in bed, she turned over to be on the bottom. I thought I had heard the bedroom door open a bit but decided to ignore it.

All of a sudden, the door opened all the way. Naked, Marcel barged in and began trying to mount me from the back.

I jumped like someone that had been hit with a bolt of lightning. I picked up my clothes and backed myself into the corner, using my clothes to cover my crotch.

Juliette jumped naked to stand in front of me, but Marcel still saw my petrified face. He stood there, naked, in front of Juliette, as if nothing had happened. He told me, "You don't need to be concerned. I know that you don't care for homosexual sex. Let me and you make love to Juliette at the same time, you from the front and I from the back."

Without speaking, Juliette signaled emphatically to Marcel that she would not take part in three-way intercourse.

Shocked at the whole scene, I said nothing and proceeded to put my clothes on. I pushed Juliette out of my way and ran toward the front door. I could not believe how fast it took me to reach my car and speed back to my apartment.

———————

Less than two hours after my return, Salwa was there again. This time, I was expecting her, although we'd made no previous arrangements. When I opened the door, I could not hide my lingering revulsion.

Concerned, she asked, "What happened?"

I let her in and again sat her down. "I do not think that things are going according to plan."

"Why?"

"This whole affair was about sex, and so far, nothing led to securing serious information about Marcel and his cohorts."

Salwa would not quit. She asked me if I had sex with Juliette. I fabricated things by telling her that Marcel showed up unexpectedly and wanted to have threesome sex. I added that I barged out of the house without saying goodbye to either of them. I further embellished the story by telling Salwa that I called Marcel a dangerous pervert.

I could see it on Salwa's face. She had mixed feelings. She was pleased that ostensibly I did not have sex with Juliette, but disappointed that by then I had extracted no salient information about Marcel's activities.

She told me in plain Arabic that I was doing so well, but she did not know what to do. She thought if she were to report to her superior without having the chance to include the details, he would stop the whole operation.

An idea struck me: I'd feign extreme disappointment and contrived anger at Juliette to get information out of her. I shared my thoughts with Salwa, and we agreed to give it one more attempt.

This time I told Salwa that I was going to invite Juliette to my apartment and for her not to come over until the following afternoon. I waited three days before calling Juliette to invite her over.

———————

When Juliette arrived, I pulled her by the arm and sat her down, clearly angry. "What do you think I am, a fool? You arranged for Marcel to come later and try to have sex with me. You are nothing but a recruiter for him and you do not mind hurting other people to accomplish your assignment and satisfy your pervert so-called husband!"

Juliette was surprised at my tone and the strength of my accusations. She crouched on the floor, held me by my knees, and begged me to understand that she and Marcel had planned nothing of the sorts, and that she took full responsibility for not checking on Marcel's schedule.

While I believed Juliette, I pretended I did not.

"What are you talking about? How could a man come into a bedroom, supposedly private, already naked, and try to have sex with another man who is having sex with his own wife? Nobody is audacious enough to do such a thing without coordinating with another person!"

Juliette swore she had no inkling Marcel was going to do what he did.

"I knew something must have happened for him to do such a thing, and now I know what that thing is," said Juliette.

"What is it? What are you talking about?" I snapped.

"He was on the hunt that evening and the girl they cornered had a knife in her possession and seriously stabbed one of his bisexual partners in the crotch. He is now in the hospital, and it turned out that the French doctor treating him is against such acts and plans to report him. The general with whom Marcel deals with is in France and he feels frustrated he cannot have the charges dismissed against his friend."

"What is the name of the general? I don't believe you," I said.

"I know who he is, but if I tell you, promise that you will not tell anybody."

I told her I did not care about anybody else. I insisted on knowing more about Marcel before she and I could continue our relationship.

She said that it was General Toulouse.

When I asked her why such a high-ranking general would help Marcel and his friends do such terrible acts, she said, "Marcel and his friends have around a hundred and twenty wineries. They offered them to the French army to hide heavy weaponry."

"I don't believe you. The army has the whole country to hide weapons!"

"The army intentionally shows itself with light weapons, which induces the Algerians to dare attack them. The army, in response, goes to the nearest winery and retrieves the heavy weaponry and ends up smashing the Algerian rebels. Nobody suspects anyone would hide weapons in wineries."

When I asked her if most of the owners of the wineries were bisexual, she said that they were overwhelmingly heterosexual, interested in raping virgin girls. I pretended to play the confused and disgusted listener. I told her that all the business of sex and bisexuality, not to mention the fact that some like Marcel would agree to his wife having sex with another man, and in his presence, was too much for me.

"I need to think about things," I said. "And I may decide the only way to distance myself from all this filth is to leave Algeria and go back to Jordan."

"No, you can't do this! I love you!"

"Love? This is not love. This is weird sex. Don't talk about love. How can I love you and know that you are married and sleeping with your husband? Who, I might add, is a bisexual rapist?"

"Listen, Zine, I would divorce him if I could!"

"You must divorce him, whether or not I am in the picture."

"But I can't." She explained that her father was in financial trouble and Marcel had loaned him money to save his winery.

Finally, I was getting somewhere. I knew of Marcel, and I knew of Juliette's father, who may not have been a rapist, but surely Marcel must have involved his winery in storing heavy weaponry for the French army. When I asked Juliette if her father was also involved in storing weaponry, she confirmed he was and then volunteered that she knew six more wineries who were associated with Marcel.

Again, I told Juliette that I needed to go to clear my head and that the whole band of rapists was overwhelming. And again, she said that she loved me and trusted me and wanted to see me soon.

When I asked why she trusted me, she said, "Once I realized you were an inexperienced lover, I knew you were not trying to seduce me to extract information from me. Attempting seduction with ulterior motives requires prior experience. You are a seducer without ulterior motives."

I said nothing, since it was a proper description of my sexual history.

———

That evening, I went back to my apartment but could not wait. I left to see Salwa at one in the morning. I woke her up to let her know the army was using wineries for arms storage. When I told her Juliette knew seven of them, she told me that my information was extremely important, but we needed the names of the other wineries involved.

She added that Algeria had over two thousand wineries, as it was the largest exporter of wine in the world. I never knew that was the case and that all the wine was produced by the French settlers.

"One way or another, you need to get hold of the list."

Within three weeks, during which time I continued my affair with Juliette, I secured the names of all seven wineries known to Juliette. They included Marcel's and her father's. We could not move forward at all. In the end, I decided to take a moderate risk.

I met with Marcel. I told him I valued his friendship but wanted him to know he and I should not have any common sexual activities, direct or indirect, at all.

"Are you willing to let go of Juliette?" he asked.

I retorted, "If she so decides, I am willing, but I have to hear it from her mouth and in your presence."

He told me that Juliette had told him that she loved me and that neither he nor she loved each other. She asked him not to take revenge, especially not taking any revenge against her father. "I believe she loves you, but do you love her?"

I told him that under normal circumstances I would say yes, but that his sexual activities confused me since he was truly a gay person, and not a bisexual, yet married to a female. This is when he said, "I am a homosexual routinely but bisexual when it comes to very young virgins."

I said that Juliette was a young virgin at one time. He said that at twenty-one she was not, and to him, young virgins were fifteen or sixteen.

"Holy God, that is too young! Where would you get fifteen and sixteen old French girls?"

"Not French, Qabil girls. We hunt them. Do you want to try one?"

"No, no, I don't want to try any, French or Qabil." He then asked me if I wanted to watch. I said, "No, watching you make love to a fifteen-year-old is disgusting."

He persisted. "You don't need to watch the rape, but you can join me and my friends on the hunt."

My heartbeat raced and my body temperature rose. I did not know what to say, and then blurted, "Only if Juliette comes along."

Marcel agreed.

———————————

The following day, I called Juliette and told her about my agreement with Marcel. I could not tell her I was seeking all the names of the rapists, yet I told her I needed to know as much as possible. Juliette was more than willing. She said that she would think about a practical way to find out everything that transpired on a typical hunt. I told her I would do the same and agreed to meet again in two days. Juliette suggested trying to tap some of the participants' phones. It was a good idea, but we had no way of doing that yet.

The hunt took place. Juliette was in agony at the selection and resistance of the young girls.

The hunt had seven Jeeps participating with eleven rapists. They were all well-equipped. The most common method was to blind the girls with the vehicles' high beams and then corner them between three to four Jeeps. Some even used a lasso to hold the girls still. By the time they finished, they captured five girls. Marcel kept his side to the agreement. He sent Juliette and me off before they raped the girls. Before I left, I had acquired the names of nine participants and five new wineries.

One of the participants, Robert, confessed that he was making a business out of the hunt. He used to recruit very rich customers from France for five hundred dollars a rape. He became a subject of interest to me and Juliette. Since he used to call France frequently, we could utilize one of his French sources to tap his phone. In Algeria itself, the phones were under the control of the army and beyond our easy reach.

This is when I told Juliette and Salwa separately that I would allocate three thousand dollars for tapping phones. Salwa let the Algerian resistance in France know our plan. Within a month, a sympathetic French leftist accepted the assignment.

At the beginning, there was not much to glean from the calls. The French technician then devised a plan where he recruited three of his comrades to fill in as interested parties on the hunt. All three flew from southern France to Algeria, courtesy of Robert. They repeated their trips three times, just to observe the hunt, and by then, we had collected the names of fifty-three offending wineries.

It took me and Juliette weeks to return to intimacy, although we repeatedly saw one another. We had been disgusted by the hunt, and she had violently vomited several times immediately afterward.

Chapter 8

I got together with Salwa and gave her all the details. She could not believe we were progressing so fast. She checked with her superior, who finally wanted to meet with me face to face.

He sat in a dark corner of a room. His face was invisible to me, while our faces were visible to him. He thanked me for my efforts and asked that we connect the dots and produce a plan to identify all the wineries involved. He reminded us Algeria had lost over a million martyrs fighting the French occupiers, and that it was the duty of the revolution to save as many Algerian lives as possible. Salwa promised him we would get together and produce a comprehensive report, on paper first, to be reviewed and committed to memory before it was destroyed.

It was the first time I heard that the Algerian revolutionaries kept little on paper inside Algeria, since the French were completely intrusive and merciless if they found evidence. They had already hung hundreds of Algerians, based on the most convoluted legal arguments. Since France considered Algeria as part of itself, the French Government, when it suited its purposes, considered the Algerians as Frenchmen.

When they were accused and convicted of treason, they would then be considered French traitors and sentenced to death. Yet, if the accused were a true Frenchman, he would be spared the death penalty.

I told Salwa that we needed a brainstorming session, so we met two days later.

When she arrived, I told her I also intended to have a similar but less intense session with Juliette. This is when Salwa asked, "Are you still sleeping with her?"

Her direct question was unexpected and out of character. After I collected my thoughts, I said, "Look, Salwa, I will not withhold anything that impacts our work, including sexual details. But to get into subjects like this, unnecessarily, why? If I'm not sleeping with her, would that mean you'd want a relationship with me?"

I didn't give her a chance to answer, and went on, "To get into a relationship with you would be the biggest mistake we could make. As much as I want to, we will be always thinking of our romance first, before we think of the revolution. Do you want this to happen?"

Salwa quieted and eventually said she agreed with me. I thought I was lucky to have squashed a potentially destructive development without any apparent ramifications. I really liked Salwa a lot, and obviously I had much more respect for her than for Juliette, but I was then driven with a focus to help the revolution, with a different private consideration for myself, which included both women.

I thought I was getting close to achieving what I had traveled to Algeria for, albeit through a different and surprising process. I focused on the reason for the meeting. Like a methodical engineer, I summarized what had happened up to that point. My second list covered the names of individuals and institutions who used such a process to facilitate or participate in the rape of young Algerian girls.

By the time we finished going over it all, we had found that somehow, we had overlooked the use of Mustafa's services. I told Salwa that once I heard about his threesome affair with Marcel and another, I thought of him as a pervert rather than one who was helping the revolution. I then asked Salwa if she could think of anyone else that we may have overlooked. She thought for a while and said that she couldn't, but suddenly she said in a low but ascending voice, "Oh, my God. Yes, there is one I never thought of, my father. He owns two wineries."

"Your father? You never mentioned that he was a winery owner."

"He is, and he has been for a long time, almost forty years. Oh, and what if he had raped my mother while on a hunt; she never shared with me the details of how it happened. Oh, my God!"

I let her process the thought aloud, and I surmised its implications along with her.

She continued, "I have keys to the house and to his safe. You see, he does not know I am in Algeria. He thinks I am somewhere in France with my mother, as she would not dare bring me back here, but she died a year ago. When he sensed that his mother was siding with my mother, he sent me two keys, one to his winery house and another to his safe, trying to prove that he loved me so much. He said that the safe contained a million francs. I still have both keys."

It took us half an hour to simmer down, and only after I had a large glass of scotch on the rocks, and Salwa had a glass of wine. We concluded that there were three sources that might provide a complete list of wineries involved: Marcel, Juliette's father, and Salwa's father.

I told Salwa that we should use Mustafa to spy on Marcel instead of Juliette, and for Juliette to spy on her own father, and likewise, for Salwa to spy on her father.

———————————

Before we met with Mustafa, we knew we were trying to involve him in an actual operation, not like the fake one of stealing a gun from an Algerian guard. We were also concerned that Mustafa was getting very close to Marcel. Mustafa was an exclusive homosexual while Marcel was mostly a homosexual.

At our meeting and before we asked him to undertake spying on Marcel, we checked him out. He sounded like he was still committed to the revolution, and with the same enthusiasm. We asked him to look into Marcel's records and get us the names of all the wineries mentioned. We shared nothing with him about the hunt, yet we mentioned the wineries in a context to encourage him to find anything he could about their link to the French army. His reactions indicated a lack of knowledge about the link.

Within two weeks, Mustafa contacted us to provide us with a list of wineries, which included eleven new names, bringing our list to sixty-four. Juliette tried to help but got caught in the process by her father. Initially, he was mad at her but quickly calmed down and provided his daughter with an additional eight names. It was an unexpected reversal of roles.

Most of the wineries involved had at one time or another been in a financial bind. Juliette's father, Maurice, told her he suspected that the French army was the one providing the loans to the financially challenged wineries, through Marcel. Marcel got a ten percent cut and pretended he was the source of the money.

"If this was the case, then Marcel would have the complete list of the wineries involved," said Juliette.

Maurice told Juliette that Marcel was no fool; he had a front, another winery owner who took care of the transactions. When Juliette asked for his name, Maurice said that he thought it was the same one who gave him the loan, Guy Antoine La Fontaine.

Juliette did not want to further pressure her father, for fear of revealing her motives. She was satisfied after Maurice gave her the names that included the two wineries that Guy Antoine owned.

After Juliette went back to Oran, she met with me right away and told me about her interactions with her father. She gave me Guy Antoine's name. It meant nothing to me.

———

Salwa told me that her supervisor wanted to meet again. He thanked me and Salwa for the eleven new names and expressed his admiration of our methodical approach and said that he was sure we could get all the names sooner rather than later.

Salwa explained to him that I managed to identify a third party whose name I had not disclosed. Her superior insisted that I share with them such name.

I immediately said, "Yes there is a third person who may be the most important of all. He is the keeper of the whole list. His name is Guy La Fontaine."

"How did you get this name?" asked Salwa, totally amazed. "Who told you?"

The way she stared at me aroused my suspicion and sharpened my intuition. As if she triggered a revelation within me, I asked in a whispering voice, yet audible to the supervisor, "Is your father Guy La Fontaine?"

"My father, my father," and she stopped, confused and not knowing what to say. Her supervisor exclaimed, "What are you talking about! Zahran is her father. I do not know of any Algerians owning large wineries."

"No, no, Zahran is my mother's maiden name. I acquired it after I moved back to Algeria, from France."

Salwa looked at me and confirmed with a slight nod that her father was Guy La Fontaine.

"His full name is Guy Antoine La Fontaine." she said, looking at me in the eye. When the supervisor told her that he did not know that her father was French, she told him that she was surprised since all her comrades knew that.

I then told them that he was the one who processed the loan for Juliette's father, Maurice, and that I believed Maurice's strong suspicion that Guy Antoine was the secret front man for Marcel and that Marcel was receiving his money directly from the French army and getting a ten percent cut.

Salwa continued, "Yes, my father's name is Guy Antoine, and he is French, and owns two wineries forty kilometers from Oran."

Salwa asked her superior if we could meet again the following day, after we processed the information. He agreed to meet after he expressed his admiration for the 'wonderful work' we were doing.

―――――――――――――

After Salwa and I discussed all the details, we contacted Mustafa and told him to do nothing. Salwa insisted that her father, under the circumstances, should be the first target. Time was getting short, and we needed the information ASAP for the revolution, as the battles were getting very heated and costly in casualties.

We again resorted to the French technician who had helped us tap the phones. He tapped Guy Antoine's phone.

In a week, the tech was in possession of Guy Antoine's schedule. He determined that Guy Antoine was planning a trip to Algiers city four days later, and then to Paris.

He gleaned additional details. Through the help of a local technician, Guy Antoine planned to disconnect his phone during his trip to Paris, to prevent the staff from relaying any unexpected incidents to the authorities. During the phone disruption, Salwa would supposedly visit her father after a long absence and would contrive waiting for him at the house. While she waited, she would open the safe with the key he had sent her previously.

The plan felt risky. I asked Salwa, "Are you as nervous as I am about the whole scheme? Don't think for a second that your father will not kill you if he finds out afterwards. He would and he would enjoy it, daughter or not. Settlers like him have a sense of entitlement and if anyone threatens such a sense, they act crisply and with vengeance. You can change your mind and should not feel you have failed if you do. If you change your mind, just cancel the whole thing without the least hesitation."

It was a make-or-break effort. Salwa proceeded as planned until one thing went wrong. With the phones disconnected, the chef at the house said he needed to go to the market to use a public phone to call Guy Antoine and tell him Salwa was there.

At first, Salwa thought of convincing the chef not to call her father but later opened the safe as soon as the chef first started for the market.

She found what appeared to be over two million francs and the full, five-page list, made up of 191 wineries. She took pictures of the list with her half-size, German-made camera and decided not to touch the money, although she was tempted to grab some.

She left her father a note telling him she could not wait for him as she had to go back to attend to her baby. There was no baby, but it was a perfect excuse, she thought. She left him with no address or phone number. When she got back to Oran, she shared the news with me. I was much relieved and so was her superior.

That evening Salwa suggested that she, I, and all the girls celebrate. When I reminded her that we should not do that since we could not share why we were celebrating, she agreed but insisted that the two of us celebrate by sharing one or two bottles of her father's premium wine that the sous-chef, François, gave her before she left the house. At my apartment, we finished two bottles, getting quite tipsy.

She slowly advanced toward me, then kissed me passionately on the lips. I reciprocated, and we engaged in heavy petting. As she was about to take off her blouse, she spilled the last glass of wine on my crotch.

That interrupted our passions and woke me up some. I went into my bedroom to change and take a shower, then came out into the living room with wet hair. She realized I had showered, and it was time to stop.

I took in her hurt look and said, "Don't you think I want it, too? I will wait for the right occasion when we do something big with the information we've collected."

She smiled and said, "I don't think so. I think you are always thinking of how you are going to tell this to Suhaila. It will sound chivalrous, withstanding the persistent advances of a desperate, young Algerian female!"

I told her she was mistaken and that while I had every intention of ending up in the arms of Suhaila, I had already decided that my desire for her was in the context of 'taking a vacation,' like Salwa had once described it.

She said, "Time will tell, since you are now searching for words not to hurt my feelings."

She explained, "The subject of our relationship is not as much on my mind as it usually is, under the circumstances. I must reconcile what I have just done, betraying my father. It is true I hate him with passion, but he is still my father, my own blood. My feelings are conflicted. The situation seems to create a theoretical challenge and a practical relief."

After watching her for a few moments, I spoke. "This time I am going to tell it to you as it is. It is up to you to believe me or not. I slept with Juliette because it was in the service of the revolution, and I will sleep with you as long as it does not hurt the revolution, simply because I desire to sleep with you. I hope you desire the same. I know what I have decided, and I will not avoid it for anything, if the time arrives."

"Yes, time will tell, but in the meantime, I respect you more than anyone I know. Keep on going; we make a great team," she said.

She turned around, looking away from me, trying to hold back a tear I'd seen glint in her eye. The situation was confusing and hurtful for both of us.

Chapter 9

The Algerian freedom fighters planned to test the validity of the list of wineries we provided them with. They asked Salwa to let me know if Juliette would tell them when her father was away, to see if the French army retrieved heavy weapons upon being attacked near the winery.

After Juliette agreed to help, I got a message that neither of Maurice's wineries were good candidates to be tested. They were both accessible from different directions.

Instead of sharing tactical details for eliminating Maurice's wineries from consideration, I told Juliette I became wishy-washy about following the so-called hunts, and I wanted to take a break. I wanted her not to suspect it was a military matter we were planning.

The fighters ended up finding a more suitable winery, one which had only a single access point. Upon being attacked by the freedom fighters, the French army went to that winery to retrieve the heavy weapons, only to find a major water conduit had ruptured and flooded the area, preventing them from transporting those weapons to the fight. It was the freedom fighters who damaged the main water conduit and made it look like a natural accident.

The exercise proved this specific winery was one used as a storage area for the French army. We checked a total of four wineries before verifying the list was genuine and accurate.

I told Salwa to ask her superior if I could participate in the next winery trap operation. She tried to convince me I had done so much for the revolution and not to feel actual fighting was the only way I could serve. I told her if successful, my participation in such a fruitful operation would be ample reason to have fun together.

Salwa knew what I was talking about. She looked at me scornfully and said, "Now, it is you who is mixing pleasure with politics and you sound confused to me. No, I will not wait for you to feel good about yourself. It has to come naturally. No formulas and no ifs and buts."

When I thought about my statements to Salwa, I realized she was right, and I was being self-centered and self-righteous. I told her she was right, and I was mistaken.

She told me I had not been like that earlier, but I had developed a touch of arrogance.

Within two weeks, Salwa informed me she had no choice but to let her superior know of my request, and she had done that.

"And?" I asked.

"And you will be on a mission soon," she said.

I ran to her and hugged and kissed her. She then teasingly reminded me not to get too excited since I could not relieve my excitement until the operation had ended successfully.

I laughed hard at her use of a double meaning.

The mission was well-planned. The Algerian fighters had intercepted news about a major French army operation against several underground Algerian fighter cells, all occurring the same night. My assigned driver—another fighter—and I were supposed to experience a flat tire in front of the winery, just minutes ahead of the French, who were retrieving their weaponry from the same winery. A dozen fighters would attack the French from the front after their weapon retrieval failed, and we would attack from the rear.

And so, it was. The fighters ruptured the main water line at the winery house, flooding the area around the house, which barred access to the weapons. The French had seventy soldiers ready to make war. Losing their heavy weapons triggered a panic, costing them twenty-one lives. I think I killed one out of the twenty-one.

———————————

Two days later, I went to see Salwa. She had heard about our successful mission. Her superior had mentioned to her how the other fighters were surprised at my performance and had the impression that I was cool under pressure.

She grabbed my head and kissed me on the lips. "I understand you were cool and collected under pressure, although you were in the line of fire. Wow, it looks like you are different in military battles than you are in romance!" she said facetiously.

I was about to humble myself and admit I was assigned one of their most brilliant fighters as my companion. He had guided me well and may have saved my life. I forgot to do as instructed, to leave once the first batch of soldiers fell. My companion had jerked my neck severely to impress on me to leave at the right moment.

Instead, I jokingly told Salwa, "I only rise to the occasion when there is a real challenge and grand prize."

She gave me an endearing, soft slap on my face.

————————————

In the evening, I bought two premium bottles of Algerian wine and a small bottle of premium fifty-year-old port. I invited Salwa to the apartment and planned to cook upside down for her, just as I had done for Marcel and Juliette. At around 7:30, as my pot was slowly simmering, there was a knock on the door.

Salwa could not wait, I thought, amused.

It was none other than Juliette. She came in all huffed up and angry. "Are you hiding from me? I knocked on your door the last three days, but no one answered. I am starting to have my doubts about you!"

I could not tell what she meant and wondered if she had developed suspicions about my ulterior motives. I had been gone four days, three in preparation, and one to execute the mission. I didn't know what to say, as I had not prepared a cohesive story about my absence. I decided my only chance was to play tough and try to pretend I was seriously mad about Juliette's attitude.

"What are you talking about? You did not even give me a chance to explain. I figured you thought of me as a gentleman and that is not the way you are sounding, as if I am a gigolo!"

As I finished my statement, the phone rang. It was Salwa. I was about to tell her to delay her arrival as my food needed more time to cook. She instead said she had to do something more important and would not be over until ten o'clock. It was the news I was waiting for, short of saying she would not make it at all.

When I went to see Juliette in the kitchen, I changed my tune to fit my improved circumstances. I told her I did not want to be impolite toward her and was trying to act in a gentlemanly way. I offered to share a bottle of wine with her, but not my food.

"The wine is my peace offering and I am denying sharing my food because of your attitude, which needs to change."

Juliette accepted the deal. We drank the entire bottle and Juliette wanted more of the same. I turned her down and asked her to leave with the excuse that I intended to have a first-class meal 'by myself, so you will appreciate that I did not care for your change of attitude.'

Juliette asked if she could come over the following day, ostensibly to make her own peace offering.

I told her she could come in four days, after she and I felt more loving toward each other, enough time to forget about our skirmish. The evening told me something new, in this case not to use the same venue for two different lovers. It was too risky.

Above all, any alienation by Juliette could cause me serious harm, since she was French. While consciously resistant to the French practices in Algeria, she could, as a spurned woman, disregard her better judgment. I knew I had to do something.

I decided on the spot that I had to end my relationship with Juliette. I also realized it had to be handled gingerly. I had no choice but to devise a plan where she would end up as a friend, without the sex part. Such a task would require a very delicate balancing act.

At 10 p.m., Salwa showed up. To my dismay, Juliette had left her scarf behind. Salwa noticed it. When she mentioned it, I told her outright that Juliette had come over unexpectedly and left after having some wine. I could see it on Salwa's face: it was a hurtful reminder to her, having Juliette visit me when she expected the night was hers.

She took time to adjust her expectations. She looked down at the floor and said, "I know you think I am mad because Juliette was here, and I was mad, but not now. I am now concerned mixing sex with politics, as someone like Juliette may be potentially dangerous."

I agreed with her and promised I was intent on neutralizing the situation before it became more challenging.

The evening's tenor had changed, all for the worse. I hesitated even opening the bottle of wine. Salwa must have felt the same. She suggested another daytime get-together to discuss removing the potential danger coming my way from Juliette. I accepted readily and introspectively. Salwa left very disappointed. I kept to my apartment, also disappointed.

In the morning, I called Juliette and asked her if she could come over within a couple of hours. She had a hair appointment and canceled it. When she arrived, I told her it was not I did not like her and desire her, but I was having problems sleeping with a married woman, and I wanted our relationship to be on a firmer basis.

When she asked what I meant, I told her I wanted to make sure Marcel was in full agreement that she was my girlfriend, that she could visit me without objection on his part, at will, and for him to cease sleeping with her.

I was hoping my demands would separate the two of us. I could see Juliette was dumbfounded at my firm demands. Once she collected herself, she said it was okay with her, provided Marcel would relieve her father of his financial obligations.

I had to think about what she was saying. As she was sitting next to me on the couch, I told her our demands were conflicted. I was asking him to lose one thing, and she was asking him to lose another. She suggested we try it and see, and if it did not work, we would have to think of an alternative plan.

I told her I was afraid Marcel might retaliate against one or both of us, after construing our request to be way beyond his level of comfort. She did not have an answer to my concern. Although it was daytime and was not supposed to be a romantic get-together, Juliette was irresistible. We ended up having two hours of gorgeous sex.

Afterward, I did not feel good about my lack of self-control. As a matter of fact, I felt depressed. I did not sleep with Salwa when I wanted to and ended up sleeping with Juliette when I was not supposed to.

———————————

That afternoon, I drank the remaining bottle of wine and a small bottle of port. The port was even more potent than the wine, which caused me to take a nap on my belly, a position I rarely assumed.

Shortly afterward, Salwa knocked on the door, but I did not answer. I had inadvertently left the door open, so she let herself in quietly. She saw the two empty bottles in the living room before she came into my bedroom. I was still sound asleep and later found I had been perspiring lightly. Salwa could tell it was not my normal behavior. She waited for two hours before she nudged me to wake up.

I got up and took a shower before I could speak coherently.

She told me why she came over and what she had observed while waiting for me to wake up. The French were making a big deal and scoring points about foreign fighters participating in the war of independence, and the FLN leadership intended to deport a couple of hundred foreign fighters, which would include me.

At that point, I felt I was ready to leave; I did not want to continue maneuvering between Juliette and Salwa. I was pleasing neither and potentially exposing myself to French reprisals all the way to a hangman's knot.

"How many foreign fighters are there in Algeria?" I asked.

"More than two hundred."

"You mean they are getting rid of all the foreign fighters?"

"The FLN leadership is feeling more confident about the Algerian struggle and the foreign fighters do not contribute even one percent of the effort." And then she added, "Except for somebody like you, a first-class spy and lover. You alone may have contributed one percent of the effort."

Her comments were tongue-in-cheek.

I said nothing at first and then told her it was not time for me to leave, and I did not want to go back to Jordan after only eight months as I was not supposed to get together with Suhaila for another four months.

When Salwa wondered what kind of arrangement that was, I told her being apart for one year and resuming our relationship afterward meant our relationship was as strong as could be. I did not share the details of my separation from Suhaila, nor did I share that she had initiated it.

Salwa eased herself further back into the couch, trying to figure out what she had just heard. She looked at me and said calmly, "I want you to disregard all feelings I have for you, or you have for me. Are you going to share with Suhaila how you feel and what you have done with Juliette?"

I stayed calm and open. I told her I had no intention of sharing anything with Suhaila except that I participated in a couple of battles. Salwa said my approach made things easy.

I thought to myself I could continue to do what I had been doing since none of it was going to be conveyed to Suhaila. I told her in principle, yes, that was the case, but I had to be selective.

"You have already been selective; you selected Juliette over me," she said.

I told her then about my ultimatum to Juliette and that I was hoping Marcel would turn down my arrangement, giving me cause to end it with her. Salwa asked what would happen if Marcel turned my request down.

I told her there would be a selection of one partner, and no other, after separating from Juliette. She did not get the jest of my statement that she would be that partner.

She added, "I hope whomever that may be, she will not turn you down after going to all this trouble."

"It would not happen by default. It had to be a conscious choice, under the right circumstances."

"Sometimes," she said, "we fabricate our own convenient circumstances."

She stood up to tell me she would be back in two days to discuss the details of my leaving Algeria.

That is when I told her I was not leaving Algeria.

She left without saying anything more.

———————————

A few days later, Juliette called and came over shortly afterwards. She told me she had already arranged my meeting with Marcel. Marcel and I greeted each other warmly and properly. As we sat around his home office table, I spoke to him openly. I told him exactly what I told Juliette.

He was not surprised at my request and said he had expected a request of this kind to come eventually, and he was ready for it. He said he would accept on one condition: I would sleep with him one time. He added it would include him having only anal sex and with no fondling or a blow job.

I was not ready for his request, but I knew he devised his request to be turned down so my relationship with Juliette would end.

I stood up silently, shook hands with Marcel first and then with Juliette, and headed toward the front door.

Juliette hollered, "Don't go. We have not finished yet."

Marcel said, "You don't have to leave. We can compromise."

I returned to my chair. Marcel said having anal sex with me was not the price of him sexually separating from Juliette; it was for forgiving Maurice his outstanding loan.

He said he did not need Juliette anymore because the hunt was doing very well and I could have Juliette, and he promised never to have sex with her as long as I was in the picture but repeated, he could not forgive the loan. "That put the ball in Juliette's court," he said.

Juliette's face turned red with anger. She stared at Marcel with protruding eyes, then burst out, "Pierre offered to pay off my father's loan if I slept with him ten times; I am going to do that and then I will be totally free and live with Zine for the rest of my life."

"Juliette," I said, "My request for you not to have sex with Marcel means you cannot have sex with any other man or woman."

She froze and said nothing.

"I am leaving," I told her. "Don't get in touch with me for two weeks, at which time you can tell me one way or the other if you can be my exclusive woman."

———————

I thought I could be out of the country before the two weeks were over, but should I delay my departure, I would spend two weeks with Salwa—even though the plans were undefined and the expectations uncertain.

The first thing I did was to add two dead bolts to my front door and install a sliding door behind the front door. I knew the walls were soundproof, but not the front door. Using the sliding door, I dampened the sound adequately. I did not want to give Juliette or anybody else a chance to overhear any conversations from inside the house.

The following day, I called Salwa and asked her over for dinner that same evening. I impressed upon her that since she was free, there was less chance the 'brothers' would assign her a task the same day and more likely they would give her a day's notice. She readily accepted my invitation.

I intended not to ask her questions, instead to share with her what had transpired with Marcel and Juliette and emphasized I had at least two more weeks without Juliette. She said I had four days, as the Algerian brothers had assigned me to a new mission. Along with me, fifteen others out of the two hundred, could stay in Algeria as long as we wanted. I was very satisfied.

Chapter 10

Once again, I fixed upside down for Salwa, made of rice, chicken, tomatoes, cauliflower, and garlic. When I turned the pot over and eased the dish down slowly, with all the ingredients steaming and stacked, layer by layer, almost perfectly, Salwa looked at me and said, "You are not only a smart spy and lover but also a great cook. This looks and smells delicious."

I told Salwa she used superlatives with all her descriptions, except when she described me as a lover.

She answered how could she say it with any superlatives since she had not tried it herself, and then added, "As of this moment, you can object in this manner to Juliette, not to me."

I told her I hoped it would not take long for her to add a superlative to my love making attributes. She said she did not intend to wait long.

I helped Salwa slice a part of the round-shaped dish and before she started eating, we both sipped on wine. I dipped my middle finger in my glass of wine and then wetted her lips with it. She liked it and she held my finger and started sucking on it.

Before we had one bite of food, she took me by the hand to my bedroom.

Three bright lights were on. She turned all of them off. I turned the dimmest one back on. She turned it back off. I told her I could barely see her body.

She said it was okay, and that I would be able to as my eyes adjusted to the darkness. In no time, she was naked, and I was naked only to the waist. I wanted to use all the techniques Juliette taught me by kissing Salwa from the neck down to her crotch, where I could suck on her.

Before I laid her on the bed, suddenly a car passed by, with its high beam on. The light penetrated my drapes, and I could see Salwa's majestic body. It was not the beauty of her body which attracted my vision; it was the tattoos that mesmerized me. They were the same tattoos she had described at the very beginning, put on by Qabil young girls, to diminish the sexual desires of the rapists.

I could not help it. I totally froze looking at Salwa's two bands of tattoos, one around her bosoms and another around her crotch.

Salwa realized I noticed the tattoos. She said nothing and stood naked, looking at me, trying to gauge my reaction. I had an inquisitive and surprised expression, but I was lost for words. She waited for half a minute, my animated but soft sexual approach suspended. She ran back to the living room, carrying most of her clothes, and started putting them on.

I ran after her in my briefs and said, "No, no, you don't understand. I am shocked you have these bands, and you were nineteen when you returned to France, too old to be hunted!"

She resumed putting her clothes on, and said, "You can put your clothes back on. I need to explain things to you."

When I finished putting my clothes on, she told me her mother developed an irrational fear of rape and even sex, which prompted her to insist Salwa be tattooed. She did it to please her mother and to attempt to alleviate some of her mother's fears.

She added, "I told you she committed suicide after she made sure I could take care of myself. Accepting to be tattooed was one of those things she thought was necessary for my protection."

I turned Salwa around and pulled her back into my hold and said, "These tattoos are special; they are the tattoos of honor and beauty. I have always dreamed of making love to you, but if I had never harbored such dreams, these tattoos would have aroused them in me."

I stood Salwa up and as she tried to undress again, I signaled to her to stop, and I took off her clothes, piece by piece. In the process, I kissed and massaged every part of her body to our fullest satisfaction. We made slow and passionate love for three hours.

I hesitantly and inappropriately told her the love making we were having was reserved for her and Suhaila only, and no other person, and then I said, "I wish you and Suhaila were one and the same; it would be the greatest love affair and love making that ever existed."

As an afterthought, I expected her to slap me on the face, having brought Suhaila's name into the picture. I realized I was wrong.

"It already is, for you physically and mentally and for me ethereally," she said, before giving me a similar massage to what I gave her.

In my case, the whole exchange with Salwa was so different than that with Juliete. In comparison, I could easily tell that Salwa acted and reacted in the most natural and loving way. She was inexperienced, just like I was, but she made love with passion and with a rhythm expressing true feelings and genuine bodily interactions.

After we finished, I held her in my arms and wrapped my legs around her.

I told her, "Don't look at me. Just listen to me. My biggest disappointment would have been making love to you without your tattoos. They define your experience, your passion and your reality and they are the symbol of your essence and a reminder to me how lucky I am to have you in my arms."

She turned around, massaged my cheeks with her right palm and reversed herself, holding me in her arms and wrapping her legs around me, and then pulling me forward to lay her head softly and pensively over my shoulder.

———————

For the following ten days, Salwa and I made love daily. After all those months, we were not needling each other about love and love making. One late evening, as she got out of bed to put her clothes on, I grabbed her and started kissing her all over her two tattoos. She told me she hated her father with a passion, and even now she could not understand how she managed to go to his house to retrieve the list of wineries that were cooperating with the French army. I reminded her she was sacrificing her feelings for the cause, and she agreed.

Once again, she said, "If I have the chance, I will kill my father without hesitation. If you knew how much my mother suffered, you would understand. She couldn't even look at a picture of a half-dressed man. He deserves to die."

I did not want to say much as I could feel how sad she was about her late mother's state of mind. On the tenth day, Salwa told me her comrade wanted to see me. When I asked who her comrade was, she said, "You know, my supervisor."

It seemed Salwa was using the wrong term, mixing it up with her supervisor at the clothing store, where she had worked in France. She told me from then on that she would call him Comrade as if it was his first name.

He asked to see me alone, specifically without Salwa. I was surprised and figured the planned mission was too secretive, and they did not want to share it with anyone except the ones directly involved. Salwa told me a similar request had happened before, involving another person and she was not concerned.

When I got to meet with Comrade, he told me they decided to accept my wish to stay in Algeria for a very specific reason. When I inquired, he said they had decided to assassinate some of the winery owners who were helping the French army and carrying out the rape of young girls.

He explained that if I could successfully execute the coming mission, it would then be time to go back. I agreed with him, provided I did not have to travel back till one year had passed from my leaving Jordan.

Without inquiring, he said my assignment would need a couple of months of preparation and should put me close to my timeline.

He added that the same person who accompanied me on the first mission would be assigned to assassinate one of the winery owners—and that I would be his partner. Without hesitation, I told him I was ready.

He said, "I am not sure you are!"

When I looked at him with a touch of dismay, he added, "We want you to kill Guy La Fontaine."

I absolutely could not believe my ears. I stood, stunned, for a couple of minutes, then finally said, "Do you realize that Salwa and I are good friends, and Guy Antoine La Fontaine is her father?"

"Yes, I realize you are close friends and also yes, she knows you are being assigned to kill her father. Why do you think she told you she wanted to kill him? To make you feel comfortable with your mission."

I did not know how to collect my thoughts, but finally I did. "Why me? Why not assign me to kill one of the other winery owners?" I almost begged.

Comrade told me it was because Guy Antoine was much more involved than the other winery owners, and when I asked how Guy was more involved, he said was selling some of the girls into several African French colonies. When I asked again if I could handle the second assassination in line, he said, "You don't understand. We know you are very close to Salwa, and she is going to help you plan the mission. A different person may not get as close to Salwa as you are now."

I knew then that they were aware we were having a romantic relationship. I added nothing as I was doing precisely what I had originally sworn not to do, to mix my personal affairs with the revolution's affairs.

I thought I had no choice, short of withdrawing all together. I decided to try to handle the situation as best as I could. Before I left, Comrade told me Salwa was eager to help, and it was up to me to use her in any effective capacity I saw fit, and I was the one directing the management of the mission, and not Salwa.

That was exactly what I had requested and pretended I was qualified to handle, but now I am concerned and nervous about the whole mission. Salwa's being the daughter and her involvement felt so strange and so sensitive.

Again, my sentiments were being tested. On one hand, I became very close to Salwa and on another I wanted to leave Algeria much more accomplished than having participated in only one mission.

———————

I was supposed to see Salwa immediately after finishing with Comrade. I hesitated since I was not ready to discuss killing her own father, even though I knew it was also her own plan and desire. In the end, I decided I needed time to think about such a new twist. I did give it some thought and decided to get together with her. I did not know how to discuss the matter.

In a delaying move, I asked her to arrange a meeting between me and my designated companion to discuss the mission. I knew he was highly experienced and wondered why he was not the one chosen, rather than me.

Salwa read my mind and told me my companion spoke poor French and no English, and the mission may entail using both languages.

Salwa then said, "I know you are hesitant to discuss killing my father; I am not. You can start anytime."

I continued to hesitate to discuss the mission with Salwa at all, at least not then.

She was very understanding and said, "I am sanguine about your mission and look forward to your success. Please stop worrying about my feelings. I can see it in your eyes. When I think of him, I don't think of him as my father. He is the rapist of my mother."

That emphatic statement went far to soothe my feelings. I told Salwa I planned to buy two bottles of premium wine for the two of us to consume that evening.

"I need the wine," I said, and she agreed.

She told me she understood and accepted the fact I was in charge, but she said she had one suggestion to make: to visit her father's house while he was away in order to provide me with the interior floor plan of the house. I told her that would be of great help.

After I thought about it, I asked Salwa why we should not consider accompanying her to visit the house to get acquainted with the ins and outs, because it would be much more helpful looking at the real thing than looking at an architectural floor plan. She told me that I was in charge of this operation and could proceed according to my comfort zone.

The next thing was to wait for the Marseille phone technician to resume monitoring Guy Antoine's phone, to find out when he planned to be out of town. Within a week, we learned that he had two possible upcoming trips. The first was one week later, to visit another winery a hundred kilometers away. We chose that time slot.

Salwa took her friend's eighteen-month-old baby with her. I cast doubt on her decision, but she said it gave further cover, because the first time she visited the winery, she had told the sous-chef that she had a baby. Her father was supposed to be the suspicious type and could have easily started doubting her untimely visits. This time, she was supposedly there to introduce her baby to Guy Antoine.

———————

We waited outside the winery until we could see Guy Antoine being driven out in the back seat and with another person in the front seat. I had been briefed that he traveled with a bodyguard, and we figured the man in the front seat was his bodyguard. We waited for twenty minutes before we went in. I was supposed to be Salwa's brother-in-law, driving her over.

Fortunately, we met the sous-chef, François, again. He said Guy Antoine had just left and insisted we stay for dinner this time.

Salwa told him we could not because the baby was scheduled for a doctor's appointment.

When François said he knew Salwa's mother, I figured he was talking about her stepmother, the real wife of Guy Antoine, who had passed away two years after Guy raped Salwa's mother. François did not know Guy and his ex-wife had never had children of their own. He told Salwa after her first visit, Guy Antoine looked all over the area but could find no trace of her.

Salwa was ready. She told François she lived in Tlemcen, a different city in the area, but she was about to change apartments and would let them know her new address, upon moving.

We both accepted cups of coffee as we roamed through the house. Salwa had a small camera and took pictures of each room, four living areas, eight bedrooms, and six full bathrooms. Suddenly, François ran toward us and said Guy Antoine was back because he had forgotten his briefcase for the meeting.

We were near the maid's bathroom. She, the baby, and I hid there. We could hear François looking for us but could not find us. I was about to wet myself but managed to hold it off. Salwa said later she wet herself.

———————————

That episode taught us a lesson. We decided to add two more fighters to the planned mission, for the purpose of watching the outside while the attempts were in progress. Guy Antoine left, again frustrated at not getting to see Salwa and his fictional granddaughter.

He had to leave for the meeting. It was most important. When I realized he could not wait to see his own daughter and granddaughter, I understood the meeting must have been an important one.

I decided not to carry out the mission before we could discern what the meeting was all about. My companion and I followed Guy Antoine the whole time. We were guided by Guy Antoine's taped instructions, having been secured by our French phone tech.

We followed him to another winery. There, we could see lots of cars, and to our surprise, one of them was Marcel's. All in all, we counted twenty-one cars. We sent for help and were teamed up with two older females, who monitored the movement of the participants at the meeting closely.

They found out it was a winery in disguise. The mansion was owned by none other than General Toulouse. When we checked with the French phone tech, he told us the meeting was arranged by none other than Guy Antoine. Days later, after the two ladies finished their watch, I went to see Comrade to report to him the results of both of our efforts. He came back to me and said the assassination of Guy Antoine was on hold until they could decide what to do with the wealth of information we managed to secure.

I had no choice; I just waited for further instructions. By then, the two weeks' separation from Juliette had finished. I knew Juliette would be over right after that, and I was correct. She hugged me warmly and said she missed me so much. She started taking her clothes off the moment she went into my bedroom, with me in tow.

I pulled my hand from her grasp. "Have you removed all the

hurdles standing between us having an exclusive relationship or no relationship at all?"

She did not want to answer, but I persisted. She said she had contacted Pierre, and he was willing to pay off the loan for only eight.

"Eight what?"

"You know. I will sleep with him eight times."

"No, no, you are not a prostitute, unless I am missing something. I will no longer accept you sleeping with anybody else. Do you hear me? You are either mine and no one else's, or you and I will have nothing to do with each other."

To cover my false unyieldingness, I told her I might be able to secure ten percent of the debt.

She said that it would not be enough, and she had no other sources for the ninety percent. She looked at me meekly and said, "Why don't you accept my sleeping with Pierre? I was sleeping with Marcel, and we were making love at the same time. What is the difference?"

I said if she did not know the difference, she should not be my woman since Marcel was her legal husband, and Pierre was just a buyer of her services, which made all the difference.

She again pressed to have sex, and I adamantly refused.

I told her that I did not have any suggestions aside from the ten percent, and for her to find a solution within three weeks, or our relationship would be over, all to my supposed utmost regret.

I wanted to give myself time to get rid of Guy Antoine, and then move out of Oran, as I did not want to hurt Salwa's feelings by having to resume sleeping with Juliette, under any circumstances.

Juliette left grudgingly, and I was relieved. As I waited to hear from Comrade, Salwa and I resumed sleeping together, but not before I told Salwa exactly what had transpired between me and Juliette.

I could see it in Salwa's eyes; she was elated at my devotion to her. At the same time, she did not want to contemplate my eventual return to Suhaila.

Chapter 11

Comrade summoned me and Salwa. He wanted to discuss the mission after hearing about the meeting between Toulouse and the winery owners. He said the FLN wanted to kill as many of the rapist winery owners as possible, but they did not want to kill Toulouse. They thought killing a high-ranking general would elicit a more violent reaction from France. The plan first called for one of the leftist French papers to publish an investigative report about the rapes by the winery owners and other Black Feet settlers, after which the mission would be carried out at Guy Antoine's house, not Toulouse's.

I told Comrade nothing had changed. He disagreed, stating that significant changes had been made.

The revised plan involved luring the winery owners to Guy Antoine's residence and assassinating them all by detonating explosives there.

Salwa asked how we were supposed to lure the winery owners from Toulouse's house to Guy Antoine's house.

Comrade said, "First, we must make sure Guy Antoine is delayed from the meeting so we can kill him while the others wait for his arrival. Once Toulouse learns of Guy Antoine's assassination, the remaining owners will head to Guy Antoine's house without Toulouse accompanying them."

I asked why Toulouse would not proceed to Guy Antoine's house with them.

Comrade said Toulouse could not travel anywhere on short notice, since he had a motion sickness, which required him to take medicine an hour in advance, before he could travel comfortably.

Salwa said the plan was doable but rather complex.

Comrade said, "At a minimum, we need to kill Guy Antoine, but ideally we need to kill everyone."

I told Comrade the plan had to include many contingencies and three backup teams, each made up of two people.

He agreed. Furthermore, he promised all three cars in waiting would have special tires to go through terrains that other cars would find impossible to navigate. I gave Comrade the description of the kind of three teams we thought we needed. He made one change and said he would take care of it.

Two days short of the three-week deadline I gave Juliette, the mission was on. It was convenient, as I could deal with Juliette depending on the results of our mission. Nevertheless, that aspect was of minor importance.

We had no choice; Guy Antoine had set the time and date of the meeting, after consulting with Toulouse. When the time came, I was shocked to see Comrade himself participating. He guided the whole mission, which pleased me greatly as I respected his detailed plans and astute mind.

Salwa showed up at Guy Antoine's house fifteen minutes before he was supposed to leave for the meeting. After she was introduced to him as his daughter Salwa, Guy Antoine received her with open arms and lots of kisses.

He paused, for he had earlier changed her Arabic name to Antoinette. But despite her name change, he resumed expressing his affection. He was exhibiting genuine emotions toward his long-lost daughter.

He lamented that she had arrived when he had to leave for a very important meeting.

Salwa told him not to leave as a friend of hers was supposed to bring over her daughter, Josephine, anytime then.

When so-called Josephine did not show up, Guy Antoine told Salwa, "What the hell, under the circumstances, I could be ten minutes late for the meeting."

Things were slowly falling in place, timeline wise. I was waiting outside, keeping François busy. Fifteen minutes later, I thanked François and directed him to go back into the separate kitchen, which was in a different building all together.

Having gauged the travel time needed for Guy Antoine to arrive, the meeting would have been thirty minutes late.

Comrade and I went into the house.

Comrade drew his revolver with a silencer and shot Guy Antoine dead.

We moved Guy Antoine's body into a hidden closet, and just as planned, Salwa and another fighter cleaned the floor of Guy Antoine's blood.

Everyone other than Salwa climbed back over the fence to the outside of the property. We needed to leave the scene while Salwa took care of the rest.

Guy Antoine had told his friends at the prior meeting his long-lost daughter had reappeared. Salwa picked up the phone and called Toulouse's house.

"This is Antoinette La Fontaine. Someone shot my father at our house, and he is dead," she said.

As Toulouse absorbed the news, he could hear Salwa wailing a short distance from the phone. It sounded genuine to Toulouse.

As expected, everyone at the meeting, led by Marcel, headed to Guy Antoine's house.

They were there in slightly over an hour. They all barged in, after Salwa had left, hiding with the team. As they were looking for Guy Antoine's body, Comrade blew up the place to smithereens.

After Salwa told us what had transpired inside, including the team having had stolen Marcel's body, we blindfolded and guided the two badly wounded chefs and the security guard out. The idea was to relay misinformation to the French authorities that there were few survivors. Among them were Guy Antoine's daughter and her brother-in-law. I wasn't sure why I requested Marcel's body be removed.

The two chefs and the security guard were kept together. Salwa and I were kept in an adjacent room. We pretended Marcel was there with us. We called his name to pretend he was there but injured. Salwa pretended she was trying to wake up injured Marcel and spoke to me as a brother-in-law, all to mislead the three into thinking that next door, she and I had been kidnapped.

The head chef was later moved to a new abandoned house, where the Algerian rebels, unknown to him, helped him free himself. When he was picked up by the police, he told them who he thought was kidnapped, and he included Antoinette—Salwa—Marcel, and me.

The head chef had never met Salwa or me, and the authorities had no record of either of us. The explosion rocked the army and the settler community. A sense of despair set on them, and they didn't know what to do. They issued statements, one after the other. Many were in clear conflict with each other.

The explosion, the scattered dead, and the mutilated bodies got to me for the first time. It dawned on me that whether it was on the Algerian side or the French, I was dealing with death and I was participating in causing death. I had to ponder about my situation.

I took a deep breath, and then nodded my head for a few seconds, wondering what I was doing. In short order, I decided that I could not at that fleeting moment, examine my stand and the morality of my actions and those of others. Just like many, I chose not to dwell on things, dismissed my self-examination, and continued to do what I was supposed to do.

———————

Salwa and I were housed in a run-down apartment. We guessed the French authorities knew nothing about us, yet we were concerned Marcel may have shared my address with some of his other friends, who were not members of the hunt. Salwa and I stayed in the apartment for two weeks; they were not the most pleasant two weeks except for having frequent sex.

The unit and our limited clothes smelled of food all the time, as that apartment was previously used heavily by a family of nine.

We then moved back to where Salwa lived with the girls. Jameela and the four girls kept kissing and hugging us. They were completely in the dark and thought we had vanished in the horrendous explosion.

By then, the girls had accepted my relationship with Salwa, and none of them made further advances toward me. I immediately asked Jameela to give me a bath and massage. She was more than happy. She ended up giving Salwa a bath, too.

While we were in the shabby apartment, Marcel's body, at my request, was carefully left four kilometers from his house, and a note was delivered to Juliette, telling her where to find the body.

He had a grand funeral. It was covered extensively by the press. Over two thousand people attended.

The papers described the atmosphere fully. Juliette looked serene, beautiful, and most graceful.

She was grieving, but for whom? Was she grieving, thinking I was dead, or was she grieving for Marcel, for whom she had no love and no respect? It took a month before Juliette was seen knocking on my apartment door, but did not knock for long. She must have thought I was dead.

We were not meeting directly with Comrade but being advised by him all the time. His third message asked that I prepare to leave Algeria, and considering the circumstances, the trip back to Almería, Spain, was going to take much longer.

I showed the note to Salwa.

She said nothing, just went into her room and started crying. I knew then I had created a bind for both of us. In my case, I had somebody to return to, hopefully waiting in Jordan. She had no one.

I wrote Comrade back, telling him there were one and a half months left to finish the year, and since the Almería trip was not going to take more than two weeks, I could stay for one more month. Comrade wrote back, telling me he wanted me safe and out of Algeria ASAP.

I was lost for a comeback. After consulting with Salwa, we could not produce anything reasonable. This is when Salwa said, "I can pretend I am pregnant."

When I asked her what we would do when the truth was eventually discovered, she said she would then claim she lost the baby. That was definitely another potential challenge to consider.

I had some qualms about lying to Comrade, but they were surmountable. Most challenging was the prospect of further complicating my relationship with Salwa. If I were to delay my trip unnecessarily, I might not have an easy excuse to participate in future operations.

I told Salwa I would agree with the lie, but only if I could engage in another operation.

Salwa approached Comrade, intending to relay the lie about her pregnancy. As she stumbled to get to the point, Comrade stopped her.

"I know why you are here. You want Zine to stay longer. It is okay with me and please do not bother about this anymore."

Salwa found it difficult leaving Comrade's room, having gotten what she wanted and avoiding the need to lie.

She relayed all of this to me as soon as she returned.

Within days, I pleaded with Comrade to give me a new assignment during the one-month grace period. He wrote to me and said the French were preparing to mount a huge campaign in seven different cities, but the details were unknown to the Algerian resistance. If I could come up with a plan to secure some of the details, he would consider keeping me in Algeria.

Salwa suggested I contact Juliette to seek information from her. It was not an easy debate, rather a most challenging decision. In the end, we both rationalized by the time I got my hands on the information, it would be time to leave, and all would be behind me.

I wrote Juliette a note, in which I told her I had been sick, and I was recovering at a friend's house. Juliette was beside herself. She wrote back and stuck the note in an old, abandoned concrete wall. She could not wait to see me and was wondering why I was not staying at my own apartment.

I chose not to address her question.

A week later, Juliette and I met at my apartment. I pretended to be in pain, nothing to do with the explosion. Then she said she knew more about me than I thought. When I asked her what she knew, I was shocked to hear her detailed answer. She told me the death of Marcel was bittersweet; she wanted to free herself from him, but she did not wish him death.

She said that as soon as she went through the formalities of his burial, she started looking for me. Frustrated, she engaged the services of a locksmith to break into my apartment. She could not find anything to indicate my whereabouts, but she found Suhaila's picture with her full name and the list of three engineering courses.

She then engaged the services of a private eye, Gilbert Simon, in Paris and told him I was an Algerian, raised in Jordan, and I must have gone to a university there, although she did not know which one.

Gilbert Simon called the University of Jordan first, the leading university there, and asked to be connected to Suhaila. After some give and take, he was told she lived in a refugee camp, and they gave him the name and contacts for the camp director.

When he called the director, Gilbert Simon claimed to represent an educational foundation which provided scholarships to refugee students. In no time, the director called him back with Suhaila's phone number at the print shop.

He called Suhaila and said he was calling from Algeria on behalf of a close friend of hers.

"You mean Suhail?" she inquired.

"Yes, Suhail, who else?" replied Gilbert Simon.

"How is he? Is he safe? Tell him he does not need to fight with the freedom fighters to prove himself to anyone."

"Don't worry, he is safe. Either Suhail or I will be back in touch."

The conversation was relayed back to Juliette. At that point, she suspected I was Suhail and had assumed the name Zine, and that I was involved in the explosion that killed Marcel. She traced my actions, and as she uncovered more details about me, her conviction strengthened. She believed I was still alive but making myself scarce.

She looked at me and said, "You don't need to lie to me anymore; I am on your side. Do you realize what my father was going through trying to secure the monthly payment to service his loan to Marcel? Toulouse did not know it, but Marcel was charging an additional three percentage points, which was over the ten percent service fee he was charging the army. Do you realize how I felt the half dozen times he made love to me, not to mention forcing me to make love to him and one of his friends at the same time? It was the only time I experienced anal sex. No, I did not want him to die, but I hated him from the depth of my soul."

After that unloading, I was sure it was worth taking a risk trusting Juliette. She told me Toulouse had helped her acquire Marcel's assets in a matter of one week. The first thing she did was to relieve her father of his debt to her as Marcel's beneficiary.

It then dawned on me. Why was her father not with the other winery owners?

It turned out he was lucky; he volunteered to keep Toulouse company while Toulouse was waiting for his pill to take effect and thus spared himself from a violent death.

She continued, "I am a rich woman now; you and I can live anywhere, in Paris, in Cannes, wherever you want."

I thought things might get easier, but instead, they had become more challenging. Marcel was dead and Juliette was filthy rich, free from any romantic entanglements with anyone else. She was ready for a clean relationship with me.

I asked myself what excuse I was left with to present to Juliette, to prevent having a permanent relationship with her.

There was none. She met all my conditions.

She looked at me and said, "You don't need to admit anything, and I do not need to overlook what I know. I accept you as you are, and you have to accept me despite my abysmal past."

I paused for a while and then found it justified to ask, after Suhaila's presence surfaced, "Now you know about Suhaila, what shall I do with her?"

"What is she to you?"

"My trip to Algeria was solely to impress her," I said. "I wanted to prove to her that I was a revolutionary, not just a wealthy engineer's son."

"Do you recall when you recently gave me an ultimatum? Either I disengage with Marcel, or you would be gone. Now, it is my turn. You have two weeks to decide and let me know. Either me or Suhaila!"

And then she left, not even giving me the usual kiss.

Chapter 12

The way my life was spinning, almost out of control, would have been comical if it were not serious and dangerous. Every time I accomplished something, the challenges of the past seemed to aggregate.

Subconsciously, I was getting numb to the fact I was impacting so many people in the process. The collateral damage I was causing was greater than the damage I was inflicting upon myself.

Despite such fleeting feelings, I was developing a laissez-faire attitude; let it be, whatever may happen.

I told myself, *take it in stride and do not begrudge what is beyond your control*, as if it were a Koranic advice, since it was all out of my hands.

Above all, I wanted to continue as I had done lately, to be open with Salwa and Comrade. I invited Salwa to my apartment, opened a bottle of wine and told her every detail I could recall, and asked her to arrange a meeting with Comrade. I could tell she was trying to reach her decisions in a completely detached manner, independent of any personal considerations.

She told me that she thought Juliette's continued feelings for me provided an ideal opportunity to have her try securing the balance of information we were looking for.

I looked at Salwa, with a clear inquiry whether she knew what she was saying.

"What? Why are looking at me this way?" she said.

I told her either she was play-acting, or she was dumb. When she said nothing, I asked, "Do you really still want me to sleep with Juliette after what we have been through together? I don't understand you."

She answered calmly. "You are being unrealistic, and I am being most realistic. One way or the other you are leaving very shortly, so why not disengage now and save the revolution hundreds of lives, instead of separating from you in a month and suffering the consequences of losing hundreds we could have otherwise saved!"

Logically, she made sense, but emotionally it was a daunting challenge. I told Salwa I would try to let her know after I had met with Comrade.

She said it was okay with her, but she expected Comrade would agree with her, not wanting anything else to interfere with the possibility of securing the information about the expected French attack.

Salwa was right, and I knew it, but I did not want to admit to myself I was vacillating because I had grown too fond of her and wanted to make it up to her in the interim, knowing I was going back to Suhaila.

Comrade ordered me to behave in accordance with Salwa's conscious advice and my subconscious fears.

He said, "Nothing should stand in the face of securing the required information, as it entailed saving thousands of Algerian civilian lives."

The fact Comrade was speaking in the thousands did register with me in a big way. I decided to put the interest of the revolution above every other consideration, and not even to take those others into account whatsoever.

I told Salwa she was right since Comrade agreed with her assessment one hundred percent. That evening, we killed two bottles of wine, but both of us refrained from having sex. It did not feel like a goodbye, but it may have been. It was strange and ethereal, and with a negative feeling.

———————

Within ten days of Juliette's ultimatum, I called her and fixed her my version of chicken tagine for an evening meal. It took some time and some quiet moments, at first, before I gave her an answer. I told her in principle she was my woman, and I was her man.

She grabbed me and kissed me passionately on my lips.

I quickly added, "But we have to be on the same wavelength politically for our relationship to be on solid ground."

To my surprise, she agreed. I added that I intended to use her to secure information for me.

"You mean secure information for the rebels?" she asked.

I told her yes, that was what I meant. I further told her that thereafter, we need not keep secrets from each other, except some unimportant operational stuff regarding the revolution.

She concurred, nodding her head.

I then asked, "Where will we end, Paris or Cannes?"

She looked at me, grabbed my face again, and gave me a passionate kiss.

Then she smiled at me. "Cannes."

I knew very well I was deceiving Juliette, as I still intended to marry Suhaila, and no one else.

I rationalized my deception as an absolute necessity to help Algeria achieve independence. That evening, Juliette and I had sex for three hours. All my ethical inhibitions were out the window, and all my pure political instincts were in play. I asked Juliette to come over in two days, at which time I would advise her what I needed to know about the French army plans.

She said she was ready for all of that and reminded me again that marrying Marcel was for her father's sake and nothing else.

I told her I believed her, and I did. I went back to the girls' residence. Although it was very late in the evening, I met with Salwa and told her Juliette had agreed to be fully cooperative and that she was still sympathetic to the cause.

Salwa looked me in the eye and said, "Is she always sympathetic or only after sex?"

I told her she was unfair to me. She had no right to make such critical comments, especially after she had encouraged me to use Juliette. She pulled herself together and apologized, claiming it was her sour mood which was driving her to make such uncalled-for statements.

We went to see Comrade to tell him of Juliette's unflinching willingness to help. He was extremely pleased and proceeded to detail the kind of information he was looking for.

He acknowledged that at least seven cities were involved but didn't know which ones, so he needed a confirmed list of those cities, and if the army's attacks would occur simultaneously or at different times. He also requested the kinds of neighborhoods being targeted and the possibility of evacuating some areas in advance. It was midnight before our meeting ended. I decided not to wait and told Comrade and Salwa that I intended to meet with Juliette right away.

Salwa, this time in front of Comrade, said, "Are you sure you need to meet with her after midnight for the benefit of the revolution?"

Comrade did not say a thing, but he noticed the comment and showed slight surprise. He asked me to leave as he wanted to speak to Salwa alone.

I went to a public phone and called Juliette. She was at home but was not feeling well and preferred to stay in bed. An hour later, I called Salwa and told her that, according to Juliette's condition, I would not be meeting with her for two days.

Two hours later, at three in the morning, Salwa knocked at my door. She told me with a regretful voice that I would have to arrange my own meetings with Comrade from this moment forward, since I would be meeting with him alone.

"I am here to apologize to you. My revolutionary spirit has been absent in the last few days. I have been acting as a spurned woman," Salwa said.

I told her what most religions and cultures lacked was empathy, and I empathized with her completely.

"If I were in your shoes, I may have even reacted violently. Considering everything, you reacted in a noble fashion."

Salwa grabbed my face, kissed me on the forehead, and said goodbye. I did not know whether that meant goodbye for good or for the evening. All what I could guess was that Comrade dressed her down big time.

Two days later, Juliette and I got together. She was still not feeling at her best. I did not want to wait, lest the French army commenced the attack. I told her what we were trying to discover.

Juliette was surprised, and she thought our requests were easy and very manageable. When I asked her why she believed they were so manageable, she said Toulouse was sharing lots of information with her, trying to get close to her. It was as if he considered her a prospective wife for his son, who was a captain in the French army in Algeria.

I could barely believe it. Again, Juliette was the object of another rival's desires. I did not mind; I thought a potential courtship could also, under the right circumstances, be used as a pretext to end my relations with her, after she would have provided the information about the pending attack.

Juliette went to visit Toulouse and, as usual, he was most welcoming. Her new suitor, Toulouse's twenty-eight-year-old son, Julian, was there. He had met her at Marcel's funeral and paid special attention to her.

She used his interest in her to collect as much information as possible, which she later shared with me.

Julian was handsome and most charming, but as stiff as they came, a typical classical right-wing officer. Juliette observed Julian and figured out those facts in short order. She intentionally directed her conversation toward Toulouse, trying to give Julian a signal of her lack of interest in him.

She opened the subject by saying she was apprehensive about the security situation in Algeria, to which Toulouse replied, "You don't have to wait long. We will shortly smash the FLN throughout Algeria, including the Sahara."

When Juliette asked why the barely inhabited region was included, Toulouse said it was one of the main weapons corridors to Algeria, originating in Egypt and going through Libya.

Juliette asked Julian if he was going to participate in the attack. He told her that surely, he would participate, but did not know where. Toulouse also said he did not know where Julian would contribute, but there were thirteen locations to be attacked, all during the night.

Juliette then asked if there was cause to worry, and that if Oran were one of the cities, she would move to Algiers city.

This is when Toulouse told her the largest twelve cities plus the Sahara were going to be attacked, all at the same time. She then asked if the army was going to warn the settlers in advance. He told her he was planning on informing the settlers one hour in advance, not wanting the news to leak to the Algerians. The French knew of their plans and were ready to entrap and finish them off, but Toulouse would personally call Juliette a full day before.

The information she collected answered all of Comrade's questions. She excused herself to go back home, as she said she was still feeling under the weather. Julian offered to drive her to her home, which she declined, telling him she had her driver to take her back.

The driver dropped her in the center of Oran, where she took a taxi to see me right away and told me everything.

I followed her surprise visit with my own visit to Comrade, but not before showing her every warm and appreciative emotion I could summon.

I hugged her tightly and rubbed my hand down her back, all the way to her bottom. I was about to massage her bosoms when I realized I was getting ahead of myself, possibly revealing my emotions were due to my anticipation to serve the revolution. I gave her a peck on her lips and left in a controlled hurry to see Comrade.

Comrade was flabbergasted at the ease and speed with which Juliette had managed to secure every answer to his questions. It made him suspicious.

I had to convince him otherwise. "I know when she is telling the truth. I know because of our intimacy. You must trust me, or you may screw up the whole thing, and I mean the whole revolution."

Comrade, surprised, looked at me intently. After a pause, he said, "I believe you. I am sure you know when she is lying and when she is telling the truth." He left right away with a smile of resignation on his face.

———————————

Due to the size and magnitude of the planned attack, Comrade had to go all the way to the top of the FLN. The news was discussed in detail. The Algerian command estimated the attack would involve 200,000 French and other conscripted soldiers. The Algerian fighters were nowhere close to the 200,000 number. Their initial plan was to preempt the French army, setting ambushes where they could. This was abandoned in short order, as they thought the French would end up overwhelming them and depleting their forces for future operations.

They deliberated, sometimes taking risks to meet. Nothing jelled until one commander said the only way this could be turned to their advantage would be for the Algerian fighters to surprise the French army and attack first. By going back to the original idea, the leadership hoped to destroy enough equipment, weakening the French and causing them to be vulnerable. They also thought the element of surprise would tend to diminish the casualties of the Algerian fighters.

Three days after Juliette visited Toulouse, Julian dropped in unexpectedly to see her. One of her housekeepers answered the door and Julian told her he was in the area and wanted to say hello to Juliette.

The housekeeper came back to convey Juliette's apology as she was still recovering. Julian said he did not intend to stay long; and his was only a short courtesy visit. Juliette did not want to unintentionally slight General Toulouse by not receiving Julian. Instead, she came out in her robe to relay to Julian that she was not ready to receive guests.

Julian kissed her hand and said as he was leaving, "I hope I did not bother you with my visit."

"It would have been perfectly all right if the circumstances were different," she said.

Julian did not want to give Juliette a way out. He said, "I am sure you will be over your cold next week; do you mind if I take you out to a brand-new restaurant? The chef just came over last month from the George V."

Juliette agreed with a counterfeit smile. She soon reported the news to me by leaving notes in the same abandoned wall, as we were not meeting in person, for fear she was being followed after asking sensitive questions of Toulouse.

————————————

The following week, Julian drove to pick up Juliette. At the restaurant, Juliette told him she was still in mourning, and it was not proper for her to see other men so soon. Julian tried to be circumspect. He told her he knew a lot about Marcel's lifestyle, and her grief was understandable, but maybe overdone.

"I know what you mean, Julian, but after all, we were sleeping in the same bed, regardless of his sexual preferences. What used to disturb me most was not Marcel's sexual orientation; it was his participation in the hunt, which eventually led to his death."

Julian seemed lost for words at first, but he then said, "They are disgusting. I know what you mean. They brought me one of these filthy young Algerians, and I adamantly refused to sleep with her. She was all bruised and cut."

Juliette asked him, "What did you do with her?"

Julian said he had to solve the problem, and that the girl's brother was with the rebels.

Juliette repeated the question to Julian's frustration.

He snapped and said, "I had to kill her to leave no trace."

Juliette was pensively indignant but chose not to show her disgust.

Julian held her hand, and said, "You know we would not do these things if it were not for the rebels. They even dare to say this is their country, and it is not ours. We have been here for over a hundred years, and we are the ones who built it. It was a desert from one end to the other."

She said it was obvious, and she was aware of it, not wanting to prolong the argument. Julian resumed trying, in so many ways, to interest Juliette in a relationship with him, but she deflected them, one after the other. In the end, Julian was frustrated and annoyed, although he tried not to show it.

What Juliette did not pick up on was how Julian knew so much about Marcel and so many other winery owners, despite the fact he had never participated in any of the hunts or benefited from them. She did not know Julian was not a regular army officer: he was a French intelligence officer.

His expertise and his desire for Juliette led him to a follow-up step: he tapped her home phone. Fortunately, as of late, Juliette was not discussing politics over the phone.

Her next call to me was all about missing me and letting me know in detail what had transpired between her and Julian.

When Julian listened to the tape, he got incensed. While claiming she was in mourning and turning down his advances, *she was meanwhile having an affair with an Algerian!*

Juliette was by far the most beautiful of the winery owners' wives and girlfriends, and Julian was on his own hunt, specifically for Juliette. He went unannounced to see Juliette and told her openly that all along he had known she was having an Algerian lover, and such was unacceptable.

Juliette got mad and accused him of spying on her and acting in a non-gentlemanly manner. He denied he was spying on her and his information came directly from Marcel before he died.

When she told him Marcel was not in the habit of disclosing the kind of relationship he had with her, Julian said he certainly did when it was necessary to lure another partner.

Juliette looked at Julian and said, "You are a homosexual also!"

Julian said he was not, but when he heard about it from the other partner, he confronted Marcel and Marcel admitted it.

She decided to challenge Julian and said, "And even if I were going out with an Algerian, what is the big deal? There are dozens of male and female French who are married to Algerians; why don't you arrest them?"

Julian suddenly stood up, took Juliette's hand, kissed it, and said, "Madame, I overstayed my welcome. Permit me to leave."

Juliette did not know what to make of such behavior; she knew it was either a resignation on Julian's part that she was not romantically interested in him, or an implied challenge to her. It turned out to be a challenge.

Chapter 13

Within a few days, Julian's taping of Juliette's phone provided him with my first and last names. When he checked on Zine Bouahmad, my assumed name, he discovered not only that 'Zine' had a flimsy record, but he was supposed to have died a year earlier. His suspicion that I may have assumed a dead man's name prompted Julian to action; he assigned two of his men to trace and follow me.

The two security men could not find me. I stayed with the girls all the time. I wondered if, due to Juliette's inquisition of Toulouse, he would have gotten suspicious, and as a result, he would surveil Juliette's house and my apartment. I had never shared the existence of the girls' quarters with Juliette.

Juliette, having decided to keep her distance from me, waiting for things to cool down, got lonely and called her father to ask him if he was in the mood to visit and stay with her. He was more than happy, as he felt so relieved of the burden of Marcel's debt.

At the same time, she kept writing me notes, sticking them in the abandoned wall. The notes were all of a romantic nature.

In the end, she wrote me a tongue-in-cheek note where she told me if she did not get to see me soon, she would hire a private eye to find me. I shared the note with Salwa, and she got permission from Comrade to let me visit Juliette, after a most careful two-day casing of her house. Surely, I did not want anyone, official or non-official, to end up locating me.

I was nowhere to be found by Julian's men, but he ordered them to look for further evidence in the apartment.

"Even if you have to break every piece of furniture and split open every mattress!"

They followed orders and stumbled upon something important. They found a scratch paper with my real name. It was written and later discarded by the movers.

I had resorted to using my real name when I found one of the two movers with the last name of Bouahmad. I was afraid they were relatives of the same person whose name I had assumed.

When Julian was given the piece of paper, he suspected Bouahmad was an assumed name, and Suhail Saber was my real name. He was not one hundred percent sure. He wanted first to check out his suspicions.

He hurried to see Juliette. She was disturbed by his habit of the unannounced visits and confronted him about it.

"I don't think you are acting properly by dropping in at will; you should have called me first."

He told her he was there on official business.

"What official business?"

"It has to do with your lover, who uses an assumed name and identity."

When she told him she did not have a lover and when she had referred to her choice to have one, she was talking in principle.

He answered she did, in fact, have one, and his name was Zine.

Juliette felt cornered and got mad. She shouted, "Get out or I will call your father and let him know what you have been up to!"

Julian, with a condescending smirk, said, "You are nothing but a call girl, marrying a homosexual for his money and then having a romance with a most suspicious and dangerous character."

When Juliette shoved Julian to get him out of the house, it resulted in one vase dropping on the floor and breaking. Juliette's father heard the commotion and got out of his bedroom, to observe a most heated argument.

He approached Julian. "You think you are a noble man? You are nothing of the sort. You hide behind this uniform to commit heinous crimes."

Juliette asked her father what he was talking about.

He explained that while others were interested in raping young Algerian girls, Julian was interested in killing the same girls who had been raped, and he was aware of at least five girls killed by Julian.

Juliette put her hands on her head in disbelief. She then went into another room, got a handgun, and returned, where she threatened to kill Julian if he did not leave.

Julian took two steps back and turned away from Juliette. When he turned around, his own revolver was pointed at her.

He fired, but just as he did, her father moved in front of her and was hit in the chest. Julian again tried to shoot Juliette, aiming at her leg, seemingly not intending to kill her. This time, he hit Juliette on the hip.

I arrived seconds after all the shooting had taken place and had no choice but to hide behind an adjacent column.

Julian was still holding his gun, aiming at Juliette. She had a gun in her hand while sitting on the floor, seemingly not knowing what to do with it.

Julian stopped for a few seconds and said, "Your so-called lover is not in the business of love. He got close to you to extract information from Marcel. I believe he is an important figure with the rebels. I will find him, and I will kill him; yes, just like I killed those filthy Algerian prostitutes."

After Julian left, I ran toward Juliette and said, "My love, let me help you. Let me take you to the hospital."

She directed me to her father, who lay some distance from her. Juliette told me her father had tried to get up but could not.

Actually, he had succumbed to his injuries without her realizing it. By then, the five house staff members were there.

One of them said in a very low tone, "Sorry, madame, but your father is dead."

Juliette shrieked. "Oh, no, I killed him! I asked him to come over. I killed him," and she fainted.

I had no choice; I could not accompany Juliette to the hospital, not after hearing what Julian had said and threatened to do. I was devastated, but had enough sense left to hurry back to the girls' apartment. I ran inside, panting, and took Salwa by the wrist into my room while the others looked on.

I told Salwa what had happened, and that Julian must have figured me out.

She called on everyone in a hurry, and said, "Collect everything you think may identify who we are, and we are leaving in less than two hours."

We spread four sheets on the living room floor and asked everyone to put the important items in one of the sheets. By the time we finished, we had filled up three of them.

After we loaded two cars with the three sheets and our belongings, we sped to a new place. The only concealed access to that place was through a dirty tunnel. It was owned by a French female settler who had left for France, to get away from the rising rebellion.

At the same time, General Toulouse called Juliette's home. One of the female staffers answered his call. Although Julian had informed him of his version of the story, Toulouse pretended he did not know any details. His inquiry centered on the news: a fight had taken place at Juliette's house. The staffer, and a close confidant of Juliette, told Toulouse Juliette's father was dead, and Juliette herself was in critical condition at the hospital, and may not survive.

She wanted to exaggerate Juliette's non-life-threatening condition, to cause Toulouse to worry as she was incensed at what had happened.

She heard Toulouse interrupt his questions and talk to Julian right then, telling him, "No, you will be transferred to Marseille. You killed one French citizen and may have killed another. Have you forgotten General Le Clerq is Juliette's uncle? He is one rank above me."

Juliette was out of the hospital in four days, and she was busy planning her father's funeral. She stuck a note in the wall, informing me that Toulouse was trying to hide Julian in Marseille.

She asked me to hide and not to try contacting her, something I was not planning to do. The Algerian freedom fighters had to assess the situation meticulously as Juliette ceased to be a conduit for information, especially regarding the long-awaited French attack. I was advised to leave Juliette a note asking her to delay her father's funeral as long as possible.

Comrade believed the French attack would not happen before the funeral. She did delay it, since she was in a depressed state of affairs and chose to use her condition as an excuse for the delay.

The funeral was scheduled two weeks later. In the meantime, Toulouse dispatched his aide to see if Juliette would receive him. When he came into her house, he took her right hand and kissed it with his head latched to her hand, bent low for a long time, almost in a gesture of prostration. Juliette told him she was humbled by his visit. She added she did not equate Julian's actions to his father's, nor did she ever consider the two of them were of the same ethical standards.

Toulouse said, "Since the death of your father, I have not been sleeping but for an hour or two, so much so I have postponed our action for another three weeks."

Juliette wanted to leave Oran for Paris to get away from all the troubles and asked Toulouse to tell her for sure if he were to advance his military campaign.

"I will come in person to see you and let you know three days in advance," promised Toulouse.

She thought his statement was strange. Either he was fully convinced she was not complicit, or he was misleading her for an obvious ulterior motive to misinform the Algerians.

When I received Juliette's note, I soon relayed it to Comrade. As the Algerian rebels could intermittently tap Toulouse's phone, with the help of the French technician, Juliette's details were helpful in clarifying some of the taped conversations. They filled in the blanks and made the picture more whole.

After serious discussions, Comrade asked me to leave Algeria for a minimum of one month, or possibly for good. I told Comrade by then it would be one year since leaving Amman.

He said he realized as much, but the revolution needed my services in Oran. He chose not to elaborate right then on what sounded like conflicting statements. Actually, they were not; he wanted me to leave Algeria but continue to serve the revolution somewhere else.

———————

Two days before I was scheduled to leave, Comrade and I met. He told me I was heading to Marseille to help in assassinating Julian. I was shocked as I had not expected to be assigned to murder anyone, regardless of his or her misdeeds. In my mind, there was a vast difference between killing in battles and outright assassinating someone.

Initially, I thought all that Comrade wanted to do was to kill another Frenchman. I thought there were others who had committed more heinous crimes and should have been given priority.

In time, I realized my thoughts were self-serving psychologically, as I found it disagreeable to outright kill someone.

Comrade told me Julian tried to convince Toulouse to take immediate action and start an expanded ten-city attack right away as he expected the rebels to preempt the French attack with a big attack of their own first. Julian was right, and had Toulouse listened to him, our side would have been in serious trouble.

Comrade thought Julian was not only vicious but smart tactically and strategically and his elimination would accomplish two objectives: punishment for his systematic killing of Algerian girls and elimination of his challenging schemes. According to Comrade, Julian needed to be stopped, preferably killed as soon as possible in order for his plans to die with him. Comrade considered him to be dangerously diabolical.

When I again asked Comrade why me, the one who knew nothing about Marseille, he said they could not secure a picture of Julian, decent or otherwise, and I needed to identify him, as I was the only one who had seen him.

Comrade told me to take an extra suitcase, this one full of Julian's clothes.

I asked why, and Comrade said they would explain in Marseille. When I inquired as to where we could secure Julian's clothes from, Comrade said that they had already done it through the Algerian cleaning lady at the military equestrian club. "Perfect samples, sweat and all."

That evening, I confided in Salwa about the pending operation in Marseille, but at the request of Comrade, I told her I could not divulge any details.

She accepted being kept in the dark very gracefully, and said, "Let us have a glass of wine together in a couple of hours."

I said, "No, let us say goodbye properly. I may not come back from this trip."

"What is on your mind?" she asked in a serious tone. I told her what was on my mind should be also on hers, or otherwise our get-together should not take place. She looked at me and said, "It will happen in four hours, after everyone goes to bed."

That night, we blew each other's bodies and minds until five in the morning. It was make-up time, peak challenge time, and possibly au revoir time, all at once.

At six, I was ready to take off, first to Almería and then to Marseille. Salwa shed a few tears as I could not hold her and hug her in front of everyone.

Somewhere close to Almería, I took the train all the way to northern Spain and then crossed by boat to Marseille. The trip took three full days.

In Marseille, I met ten Algerians and one Frenchman; he was none other than the phone technician.

The following morning, the technician introduced me to a man who bred and trained search dogs, something he learned as a prison guard from the Nazi army units after their defeat. He told me why I carried over twenty pieces of Julian's clothing. As we did not know Julian's whereabouts, the clothes were for the dogs to smell and trace after we identified the general area Julian lived in.

I would have to accompany the dog handler so that I could positively identify Julian once his dogs tracked him down. At the same time, we didn't want me to be recognized. I was sent to a barber shop for a beard and thick glasses, which transformed my appearance.

It was all well-organized. I was taken to the very basic and shabby offices of a French Marxist paper. There, one of their artists tried to do a sketch of Julian's face, with my help. I was impressed with myself and the artist. After the artist finished, I thought the sketch was much better than expected. The sketch was scheduled to be shown to around 2,000 other leftists.

It was the 792nd interviewee who said he had seen Julian in Vieux Porte.

———————

On the third day of our active search, we struck gold at a sailors' bar.

Julian was in the corner, and to my surprise, he turned out to be bisexual. The bar was participatory all the way; the customers and the servers had episodes of sex, as they were eating and serving. Julian was passionately kissing men and women. That night, the bar was crowded and dark; it was not easy to figure out how to proceed.

I told the dog handler I had lots of money. He then suggested we reserve a private room, which we did for around twenty dollars. The room was on the way to the bathroom. The plan entailed the dog handler and two dogs wait in the gallery and then for the dogs to force Julian into the private room.

Julian was on his way to the bathroom in fifteen minutes, when the dogs were made to jump him. Armed with a gun, he shot a dog and fled. He did not figure the dogs were search dogs.

The remaining dog was made to smell more of Julian's clothing; it led us to an old building. The dog followed the scent to Julian's apartment. We expected Julian to use his gun again. The dog handler also had a gun.

When we managed to open his apartment's door, I spoke and said, "I am Zine. I know you killed innocent young Algerian girls, and I am here to settle the score. This has nothing to do with Juliette or her father."

He said, "Come in. If you are a man, and try to settle your score, you will die first."

I took an empty soda bottle and threw it deep into the apartment, toward the area his voice was coming from.

The dog handler let the dog loose, after hearing the shattering of the bottle. Within seconds, the dog handler had his intense-beam German flashlight on, to observe the dog grabbing onto Julian's arm, the same arm he was holding a handgun with.

The group had been instructed to try to extract important information from Julian and were given twenty-four hours to accomplish that before killing him.

Although almost blinded by the beam of the flashlight, he tried to aim at me and took a shot. It hit me right above my heart. In response, the dog handler shot Julian, hitting him in the hip. It appeared the handler intentionally did not want to kill Julian.

———————

When I woke up, I was in severe pain, in an underground wine cellar. One of the ten Algerians was a medic. He tried to help as much as he could. I needed a surgeon, and we needed equipment for the procedure as I could not be taken to a hospital for obvious reasons. I still had plenty of money which I kept in a secret pocket on the inside of my slacks.

When I took the money out of my pocket, everyone here was looking at each other; it was an unheard-of sum of money for them. I then told them about my father, and for them to contact him and let him know I was hit and needed medical help.

They called my father in Kuwait and explained to him the situation in detail. He wanted to call back, but the Algerian caller told him they were using a public phone, and they would call him back in a matter of hours.

My father called the deputy prime minister of Jordan, who was once my father's college classmate. He then reserved three seats on an otherwise full flight, from Kuwait to Beirut and then to Paris. The other two seats were for two surgeons, one of whom was my father's cousin. They carried ample medical supplies but could not carry anything except four small pieces of medical equipment. In three days, they were in Marseille.

In the meantime, the group had secured all the equipment the surgeons needed. I was sedated and unconscious most of the time. When my father and the two physicians arrived, they found me to be in bad shape, but to their surprise my vital signs were fine. I was laid on a billiard table for the procedure. It went well. I could not talk to my father until twenty-four hours after the procedure. I was out of commission for one week.

My father had arranged for my transfer to Kuwait as he was confident it was also my intention, considering my health situation.

I told him I still had things to do in Algeria. He did not try to force the issue. He told me he was proud of me.

He called my mother and told her about my decision. As usual, she said I did not know what I was doing and asked my father to find a way to force me to leave Algeria. My father was open with her. He told her he found me to be a true man and respected my decision and he did not intend to do anything else, even if he was able to force me to leave.

Julian was a heavy smoker. He promised to give the group one piece of information for three cigarettes. He was true to his promise. He told us his father was not going to command the attack; it was General La Pierre. That gave the Algerians the opportunity to spy on La Pierre.

Julian told them he was willing to die after chain smoking the three cigarettes.

The group was surprised as the twenty-four-hour deadline was about to expire. They met and held a five-minute tribunal, where all of them decided to execute Julian.

Before he died, he revealed that he had killed twenty-one young Qabil girls. They did not ask for my own vote as they told me I was too sick to pass judgment. They executed him in front of my eyes. It was my first experience of this kind; it was not pleasant, nor did it feel satisfying. I felt a void after I saw Julian's limp body fall on the floor.

Chapter 14

My father had bought me an open first-class plane ticket to accompany him back to Kuwait.

I told him I intended to exchange the ticket for a different itinerary, depending on the circumstances. I repeated I had still unfinished business to take care of in Algeria which would take me another two weeks.

When I asked him about Suhaila, he said the first thing he would do upon my return, was to take me back to see her. It was an attempt on his part to see if this kind of news would change my mind.

When I said I had to stay in Algeria for at least two more weeks, he asked for some privacy and took a letter out of his briefcase.

It was from Suhaila, addressed to me.

I thought it was written just before my father left to come over. No, it was a letter she wrote three months after I had left for Algeria; it was delivered to my mother and my mother never read it or sent it to me, although I had sent her and my father my mailing address.

In it, Suhaila said a dozen times how much she missed me, yet, she said, she had to wait for the promised one-year period.

When I asked my father if that was it, he pulled out another letter, delivered to my mother two months after the first one. Suhaila mentioned the five months and said she still could not sleep at night and her love for me had increased. He then pulled out a third letter. This one had a picture of Suhaila at a gathering attached to the letter, and it was written and delivered two months after the second one. Unlike the other two, it was only a one-page letter. The letter said:

My love,

This is the last letter I will write to you, and I hope you will get to read it. Your mother assured me that if I ever became your wife, it would end your relations with her, and as I told you before, this would be unacceptable to me. As such, I have decided to get engaged to Musa; you know him, he is another engineering classmate of ours.

I wish you all the happiness, and the warmth and love of your father and mother.

Your friend,
Suhaila.

I looked at my father with total shock and said, "Is this the last letter?" He said it was. I covered myself and said, "Fuck this life. Why? Why is this happening to me?"

My father then explained to me, after I stopped hyperventilating, that when Suhaila delivered the second letter, it was received by one of the housekeepers. Upon my mother receiving the letter, she became totally enraged, sped toward Suhaila, and slapped her on the face and told her she was a low-class, shameless, and conniving girl.

My father added, "How could a self-respecting person accept this? I don't blame Suhaila one iota, and she made the right decision; your mother is impossible to accommodate. She has severe paranoia, and we must face this reality."

It was the first time I had heard of my mother being described as paranoid. After I calmed down, I asked my father if he was sure of the diagnosis. He said he had consulted with half a dozen different psychiatrists, and they all agreed she was severely paranoid. I asked what I could do under the circumstances.

He said since Suhaila decided that she and I both had to have a relationship with my mother for her to marry me, I could do nothing and had to abandon the thought of getting back with her.

"But now, it is too late; she is a good girl, but she is engaged to Musa. Forget about her," my father said.

I felt like a useless and aimless person. My father and the two physicians tried to take me out of my hiding to enjoy Marseille, but I refused to join them. I was in bed sulking, with fleeting delusional thoughts of living by myself on a desert island. I felt like I was disengaging from the world. As an afterthought, I knew the shock would have been much greater if it came without our year of separation.

Subconsciously, I knew there was Salwa and even undependable Juliette in the picture. What challenged my ego even more was the fact Suhaila had closed the door on any chance to fix the situation, by getting engaged. It was a total rejection, and an affront to my commitment to reconnect with her, not to speak of the fact my Algerian trip was for the purpose of impressing her and confirming my attitude being opposite to my mother's. I had also hoped to reveal myself and dispel the image of my wealthy status.

One of the Marseille Algerians, not knowing much about my state of mind, told me I was recuperating fast from my procedure, and Comrade was looking forward to seeing me in Oran. At that point, I wanted to get lost somewhere in France, but thought it was my duty to go back to Oran. I figured the challenges of the revolution would take my mind off my loss of Suhaila.

———————————

I arrived on the evening of January 31, 1962. Without having been forewarned, the city was ablaze. The Algerian fighters had initiated their offensive, anticipating that the French forces would commence their own operation within twenty-four hours.

It was not easy to get to Comrade, so I met him at a brand-new location. To my surprise, Salwa and all the girls were there, including Jameela.

Jameela winked at Salwa, then ran to me and hugged me, careful of my wounds.

"You are a lion, one of a kind," Jameela said. I did not feel like it.

They all had heard I got shot and almost lost my life chasing Julian. Salwa could not wait. She signaled to me to move to a secluded corner. She grabbed me and kissed me on the lips passionately. She said I made her proud. Despite the fact I had planned to leave and reconnect with Suhaila, she was just most proud and grateful to have known me.

I told her, "Suhaila is no more. My mother made sure of that, and Suhaila accommodated her."

She asked that I explain myself right away, and she could not wait for later in the evening to find out. She added the situation was very fluid and at any moment she and I could be in two totally different places, doing separate things.

I told Salwa that Suhaila had gotten engaged to another classmate of ours, and it was all over between her and I.

Salwa did not know what to say. She just kept staring at me. I thought she was confused. She wanted me for herself, but felt sorry I, someone she cared for, had my heart broken. Comrade showed up and broke up the conversation.

He told us that Toulouse had been in touch with Juliette for the last two days, having sent her a messenger, and Comrade wanted to know what he'd told Juliette. It was for me to find out.

I told Comrade I owed Juliette a visit and was ready to head to her house.

He said that at the start of this Algerian campaign, all routes had changed, and I needed to be guided by someone familiar with the detours. Salwa again questioned my motives, unsure if I wanted to satisfy an existing burning flame, or if they stemmed from a genuine call of duty.

I surely did not want to be presumptuous, expecting Salwa to accept me unconditionally because Suhaila dumped me.

Given the chance, I took Salwa to the side and said, "Now, it is only you, if you think I deserve your companionship. I know I don't seem to have behaved as expected. I believe I did but my circumstances were and still are challenging. I know one thing: if you accept me, you will be the one and no one else."

"Go see Juliette," said Salwa.

"Yes, I will see her, but rest assured it will be about the imminent freedom of the Algerian people and nothing else!"

Salwa paused and said, "You will do what benefits the struggle, and please do not get too ethically sensitive at the expense of our efforts on behalf of the revolution."

———————————

It took twice as long to get to Juliette's house as it used to. I had to maneuver to avoid both the Algerian rebels and the French Gendarme. The Algerian forces were attacking the same posh area, where many French officers lived. They were all around. They alternated placing their forces on the ground, in some cases and on the roofs of the French villas, in other cases. The idea was to establish visual control of any advancing French forces.

When I got to her house, there was one housekeeper left there. She said Juliette left when the shooting started, and she gave me the address where she was heading to. Again, it took twice as long to reach Juliette. It was her father's friend's house.

When Juliette saw me, she was shocked. She did not know where I had been, and what had happened to me.

She hugged me. Accidentally pressing on my stitches, she could see I was in some pain. As she opened my shirt, she noticed the bandages wrapped all over my torso.

She tried to make up for lost time, but I told her I could not, due to my injury. My answer did not satisfy her as she thought I could have at least tried. She complained she was waiting for me, not knowing where I was, and here I was not even trying to be romantic.

This is when I intentionally snapped at her, as I wanted to arrest all her attempts, since I had no plans to engage sexually with her. Salwa was the one I'd chosen, although I had never received a definite answer from her.

I looked straight into Juliette's eyes and said, "Do you hear yourself? Oran is burning; you are in danger yet only thinking of sex. I am here to save you from danger and possibly from death. The Algerians have no plans to hurt innocent civilians, but the leadership is not always in control of the situation."

My admonition brought Juliette to her senses.

I told her I was there to make sure she could get out of the country.

"What about you? Are you trying to get rid of me? You only talk about me. How about us?" she asked, looking at me with genuine concern and trepidation.

After a lengthy argument, I convinced her the house she was at and all the other houses she was considering sheltering in were not safe. She relented. Yet, she insisted on first going back to her house to fetch her clothes, jewelry, and cash.

I had no choice, as we were wasting so much time. My guide said it was getting extremely dangerous, and he would try to have a couple of fighters join us on the way to Juliette's house, and so he did. It took us over an hour, stuffing clothes in suitcases and boxes. Juliette opened the safe to get the cash. It was a huge walk-in safe with thirty-centimeter steel walls, which could house around forty people.

When I looked in, I could see tens of millions of French Francs, all courtesy of Marcel's hunt parties' largess. The money brought back to mind the tragedy of the rapes. Although the winery owners' hunts, which were started and nurtured by Marcel, comprised a small part of the big rape crimes through 132 years of French rule, I could not help but recall and gloat at my contribution toward Marcel's death.

Within seconds of opening the safe, we could hear noises coming from the garden, and in no time, there was a loud knock on the door. They were French soldiers. Juliette hurried up and shoved me and my three companions into the safe. She showed me the button that opened the safe from the inside, just in case she was taken away. Then she ran to open the door. It was a French army captain and nine other soldiers. The captain apologized and asked to speak to Juliette's husband.

She told him he was a martyr in a ghastly terrorist explosion. After he apologized, he told her the rebels had been witnessed in her neighborhood, and they were hiding in inconspicuous houses as housekeepers and other kind of helpers, and as such they had to search her house.

She pretended to welcome his search, and in due course he

asked her to open the safe, to which she said she wished she could as her husband died without leaving behind the combination. When he said he would blow the safe open, she told him the walls of the safe were thirty centimeters thick. To her relief, he changed his mind. It was a close call which ended up with the soldiers finding no one, and nothing aroused their suspicions about Juliette. They left soon after Juliette served them lemonade.

When Juliette got to open the safe, she could see the utter relief on my face. "Oh, my God, you were so pale a minute ago. Your face is gaining its color second by second."

In the meantime, as I moved deep into the safe and beyond the gold, cash, wine, and crystals, I discovered a compartment. When I searched it, I found a cache of weapons beyond my wildest expectations. It was made of rifles, machine guns, and bazookas, with plenty of ammunition, enough to arm over a hundred fighters.

The discovery of the weapons immediately changed my priorities. I knew if I could get those weapons to the Algerian fighters, they would make a huge difference in Oran. I needed to find an easy way to tell Juliette about my intentions to deliver the weapons to our fighters as soon as possible. I forewarned my companions that Juliette would say no, and instructed them to be ready to act decisively. I thought the weapons were too important to leave behind.

As the four of us got out of the safe, she resumed stuffing cash in five different suitcases. She barely managed to stuff five percent of the cash, and she left all the crystal and gold behind.

As she was about to close the safe door, I stopped her. I asked if she knew what was there in the safe beside the cash, crystals, and gold.

She said, "What does it matter? Nobody can open this safe unless they blow it up with large explosives. Everything will be here when I come back."

I took her by the arm and showed her the cache of weapons. I could tell she was shocked. I clasped my hands behind her neck, pulled her toward me and looked her in the eyes and said, "Juliette, can you imagine how much those weapons could help our fighters? They could make all the difference, especially the bazookas. I have to see to it they are delivered as soon as possible; my companions will make sure you will safely leave the country."

This time, she did not react angrily. Instead, she looked at me with some resignation and asked, "I have the feeling you don't mind sacrificing anything and anyone for the liberation of Algeria, including me."

I then took a posture I learned from Julian: that of a slighted aristocrat. In reality, I did not have the answer to her statement. I said, "You really know how to insult a man. I don't want you to leave on a sour note. I will say no more."

I asked Juliette to give me the combination to the safe and promised her we would not touch anything but the weapons. I successfully opened the safe twice.

The last time she locked it from the inside, she took off her clothes. When I opened the safe again, I did not attempt to resist. The cache of weapons was too precious not to have. We made love twice. I thought it was a sensitive exchange, but all too unavoidable, sex for saving lives. I knew my promise to Salwa was shelved under the circumstances.

Within an hour, Juliette was on her way to Almería first and then to Paris, through Madrid.

Chapter 13

After Juliette left, I was left alone with one of her housekeepers, Michelle. I did not want to gamble by calling any of my contacts. We knew the French authorities were trying to tap as many phones as their available technology allowed. After all, the number of phone connections was very limited at the time. I did not know how to go back to see Salwa or Comrade.

I asked the housekeeper if she knew her way, and she said she had lived in Oran all of her thirty-six years of life, and she knew it abundantly well. I was loaded with dollars but decided to take ten thousand francs from the safe and keep them with Michelle. While Michelle knew her way well, neither she nor I knew where the French forces positioned themselves.

Seven kilometers into our walk, we tried to cross a wide dirt road. The road was wet and muddy, through and through, over a meter deep. I told Michelle to be careful and to tread lightly, stepping over areas with broken branches, as they reinforced the ground. She did not listen to me and decided to sprint across the muddy wide road.

Suddenly, she sank in the mud all the way to her waist.

Her drop into the muddy surface pushed her bag out of her hand, yanking it four meters in front of her. I looked at a scene I had not expected, with Michelle's bag, which contained her money and ID, on the muddy surface, sinking. Michelle herself was desperately stuck in gooey and sticky soil.

Surely, I did not want to get stuck myself. I scrambled to the other side, where I climbed a tree that hung over the area where Michelle was stuck, and tried to pull her out of the mud. After trying unsuccessfully to use several dry and fallen branches, I found one long and stiff enough to pull Michelle out. Slowly, Michelle got out, but not before her slacks were pulled off by the mud.

There was Michelle, from the waist down, in her underwear. It was impossible to retrieve her slacks, but I retrieved Michelle's handbag. I waited until it got dark before we resumed our journey.

———————

Michelle steered us through back roads, usually left idle by the French forces. Suddenly, we were confronted by a French soldier drinking wine. It was far from being a suave scene. The moment the French soldier pointed his rifle at me and Michelle, she peed in her underwear. Yet, that may have saved our hides; the French soldier started laughing and pointing at us.

He told me I had to screw Michelle through her urine and then asked rather politely if he could screw her himself.

I intentionally ignored his request and said, "What can I do?" But I told him I had a present for him.

When he asked what kind of present, I took two thousand francs from Michelle's bag and gave it to him.

He was most thankful and pointed to an empty bottle of wine he had tossed on the ground and said now he could buy lots and lots of wine. I suspected he was an alcoholic. He let us go without question.

At around 10 p.m., I knocked on the door of the hideout where Salwa and the girls were. After they checked us out through half a dozen beeping holes, they opened the door. The look on their stupefied faces was almost scary, as if they were looking at two ghosts.

While they could see my muddy slacks and bruised face, as a result of my hanging down from the tree trying to pull Michelle out, several of them were focusing on Michelle's underwear. I told them to stop it, and I would tell them the whole story after Jameela gave me a bath. I needed it, as the sandy mud had gotten into even my nostrils. When I got out, Michelle had already cleaned herself and put on one of the girls' more fashionable dresses.

I told everyone our story on the way here, in a shortened version, and asked if I would speak to Salwa alone. While everyone thought it was a romantic get-together, I told Salwa about the arms at Juliette's house.

Salwa immediately dispatched someone to inform Comrade, and within two hours the same person came back accompanied by twenty fighters. They only had a few handguns and a couple of machetes on them. They were instructed to accompany me and Michelle back to Juliette's house, to fetch the bazookas, the main item the rebels were short of.

Comrade did not mention Salwa; she decided on her own to accompany us, carrying a handgun.

On the way, Salwa could not keep her distance from me. Even some of the fighters noticed her soft posture toward me. She got close and whispered in my ear that she could not sleep the past two nights, thinking about me and about being exclusively in my life.

I told her I was worried, but I wanted to share with her something she should know. She said she did not need to know anything, and she was in the clouds considering our relationship.

We arrived at Juliette's house at five in the morning. I opened the safe and led everyone to where the weapons were stored. I had forgotten a most important thing: the blanket Juliette and I made love on was still there, on the floor of the safe. Salwa looked at it, rushed out of the safe and went into an adjacent room and started crying.

I ran after her, knowing what had taken place and wanting to explain to her the blackmail conundrum I was in, and the benefit to the revolution I had to take into consideration. As if things could not get worse; they did and always managed to find a new bottom. While I was placating Salwa, Juliette came into the house with her companions, smiling and shouting that the boat's motor would not start. Juliette's voice alerted everyone, most of all Salwa. She got out of the room and witnessed Juliette coming toward me, with her hands wide open, meaning to hug me.

I had to think fast. "Stop, we are all getting out of the house right this moment. They are dismantling some ammunition that may totally blow up the house," I yelled. "Everyone, get out, except for those handling the weapons and ammunition in the safe."

I ran out, and everyone else, including Salwa and Juliette, ran out as well.

I saw Salwa and Michelle go the same way, so I went the opposite way, turned around and went into the house from the back. I joined the twenty-four fighters and Juliette. I thought after my alarm call, the safe was the best place to hide.

I waited for a mere fifteen minutes, since I did not want to take longer and have Salwa and Juliette get to know each other and exchange tidbits about my relations with each of them, or to have the two argue about their sentiments toward me.

I went onto the balcony and announced all was clear. When Salwa and Juliette came back in, I could see both may not have exchanged anything, but both had serious questions on their faces. I took the initiative and introduced them to each other. I told Juliette that Salwa was heading the transfer of the weapons. I wanted to make sure the less predictable Juliette would not criticize or possibly attack Salwa.

I told Salwa that Juliette was kind enough to readily contribute the weapons to the revolution, all gratis.

I added circuitously, "…but sometimes Juliette extracts small favor, to feel she was not giving them free of charge."

Salwa understood what I meant.

Juliette looked at me and said, "No I don't. I don't know what you are talking about."

I had again to think fast, and I said, "It is nothing. It is like we were not charging you for your trip to Almería and we were providing you with helpers to carry your belongings, also free of charge."

"Are you asking for forgiveness?" asked Salwa.

"Oh, no, there is no need for forgiveness since it was all in the service of the revolution and after all, it was all under duress."

Juliette could not follow the give and take between me and Salwa. Before I started to tell Salwa she needed to go to the safe to approve things, Juliette grabbed my arm and said, "Let us continue what we started; I may have some weapons in my bedroom."

"Oh, then you can take Salwa with you; she is handling the weapons."

Juliette looked at me, mad, disturbed by my rejection and said in a gruff manner, "She is the wrong type."

I looked at Juliette and said, "We are here for one purpose and one purpose only, to be hindered by absolutely nothing. We are here today to retrieve the bazookas and do nothing else."

Juliette got madder and was almost oblivious to the fact Salwa was present, looking at her and listening to the conversation.

"Then I will stop the work in the safe until you personally look for the weapons in my bedroom. Otherwise, I will stop the transfer of the weapons altogether."

I had to do something decisive. I grabbed Juliette's arm firmly and whispered in her ear, loud enough for Salwa to hear.

"Don't be childish, and don't be stupid. If you try to stop those fighters, they may chop your body into little pieces and feed it to your dogs. Do you understand how much these bazookas mean to them?"

I could see the shock on Juliette's face and the fear in her eyes.

Salwa made the slightest smile, enough to signal to me she agreed with my tactics.

It was an encouragement, which prompted me to add, "Look, Juliette, you don't seem to appreciate what is happening in Oran. We all could be dead by tomorrow morning. My only concern is our safety. That includes the transfer of all the bazookas, and to that end, I do not want anything to interfere with this objective. I suggest you find something to do in the meantime. Otherwise, we will be in deep trouble."

Juliette went huffing to her bedroom.

Salwa looked at me and said, "Now I understand and appreciate the situation. I was afraid if I went into her room, she would try to make a homosexual out of me!"

"No," I said, "that is her husband. She is just an oversexed heterosexual."

Salwa said again she understood the big picture and now she believed I was working for the benefit of the revolution through and through.

Then she added, "I have to confess, although she is definitely off center, she is stunningly beautiful, and I don't blame men for being attracted to her."

"True love entails meshing not only two bodies but also two minds and two souls," I said. "That ensures there is a natural and complete movement of affection both ways, between one companion and another."

Salwa took her index fingers, put them on her lips, then on mine and said nothing. Little did she know, Juliette saw her gesture.

I did not know why Salwa risked doing this, other than perhaps she felt I was honest with her in my description of my relationship with Juliette. Based on what she had observed of Juliette's personality, she seemed to think that Juliette's kind did not fit my aspirations. She was right.

Juliette had to decide whether Salwa's finger-kiss was romantic or not. It did not take her long to ascertain that it was romantic. It was almost as if Salwa pushed me against the wall and gave me a real kiss on the mouth.

Saying nothing, Juliette went to her room and called Toulouse. She described the fact we were at her house and asked for help. We were lucky as impetuous Juliette came out and said Toulouse was dispatching French troops to arrest us. I didn't need to guess what brought that about.

I looked at Juliette and said, "I know what you did is against your beliefs, but your sexual desires took over your better sense." I then ordered her to be tied up.

She hollered and cussed, kicked, and bit, yet I was intent to subdue her, as I needed time to figure out what to do.

Salwa approached me and apologized. I told her we did not have time for apologies. We needed to leave right away.

All together we were twenty-five men and Salwa. Salwa took over the command of the situation. She asked that only fifteen fighters load and transport the bazookas to the fighters in the city. Another four were ordered to stay back, each keeping two Bazookas loaded, to use against the advancing French armored cars.

In doing so, Salwa put more value to saving fighters and civilians in the city than herself and my own life. Both she and I could easily appreciate the many hundreds of Algerian lives the bazookas could save.

An additional two fighters were assigned to be snipers, and three more were ready with machineguns, all retrieved from the safe.

As the fifteen with the loaded bazookas were about to leave, we could hear the French armored cars approaching Juliette's house in the distance. I could not think fast enough. That prompted Salwa to act on the spot and rearrange things. Salwa asked seven of the fighters to squeeze into one car and another eight to squeeze into another, to try to leave before the French arrived.

"It is risky, but I have to do this," she said.

I did not know what she meant.

She ordered the fighters to tie Juliette to the hood of one car and Michelle to another. While surprised, I said nothing. I knew Salwa was much more experienced than I was. We and the fifteen fighters left in three cars, with her and I alone in the second. The car Juliette was tied to went first and the one Michelle was tied to went third. Ours was in the middle.

The French troops were a hundred meters behind us when the fighters in the third car brandished several bazookas toward the French soldiers and threw them a note wrapped around a rock. It said if they started shooting, we would then kill Juliette and Michelle.

They refrained from shooting but kept following us. We put three kilometers between us, but we grew concerned since the terrain was getting challenging for our special cars, but not for the French armored vehicles. As we kept increasing the distance between us and them, we passed by a ranch.

Salwa stopped the cars, surrounded the ranch, and proceeded to tie up the French rancher, his wife, and his three workers. Then, she asked five fighters who were experienced with horseback riding to get out, mount five horses from the ranch, and loop back behind the French forces and attack them, while the rest of us looked for a sheltered position to confront and defend against them.

Once again, Salwa managed to take quick and much-needed tactical action.

In less than seven kilometers, our cars could not go further as we faced a hilly area. There, we were joined by seven Algerian rebels who happened to be in the vicinity. They were stuck, too. We got out and prepared for the French forces. We had enough time to load four more bazookas before the French arrived and stopped 300 meters away. We untied Juliette and Michelle off the two cars, and Salwa even apologized to them.

The five on horseback were less than two kilometers behind the French forces. We initiated a defensive action and hit one of the seven French armored vehicles. Our horsemen got close to the French in a matter of seven minutes. Unexpected by the French, they attacked and disabled two more vehicles.

To our surprise, the French, with four vehicles left, with-drew. Salwa approached Juliette and Michelle and told them they would be released whenever we got to a safe place. She told them they should not call the army anymore, and if they did and we got to know about it, they would become future targets for assassination. Juliette was not cooperative. She spit in Salwa's face.

Michelle, however, promised not to tell.

Salwa told Juliette she would not be released but possibly would be used in a prisoner exchange, although Salwa knew the French harbored no inclination of exchanging prisoners with the Algerians.

True to her promise, Salwa released Michelle before we got back to one of our hidden locations. When we arrived, Salwa arranged for Juliette to be transferred to a different group of fighters in a different city. I did not know whether that was a practical decision or a romantic one.

Salwa and I thought we were finally ready to celebrate our own success in defeating the French force and securing a cache of bazookas, to be used all over Oran against the French armor. We did not realize how much we were cut off from what was happening all over the city of Oran.

When we returned, Comrade was waiting for us. We expected him to congratulate us warmly. Instead, he looked sad and grim. He summoned everyone and told us Oran had been held by the

Algerian freedom fighters for three days, but now the French had turned the tide, and took back most of the city.

He said many freedom fighters had been killed or captured, and others were fleeing and hiding in places unknown to the leadership.

"We have to build back everything, if we can first avoid the wrath of the French forces. I want you to be ready to move on short notice, with two important priorities. The first is to hold on to the precious bazookas, and the second is to secure cash, as many are without jobs and income, hungry and desperate."

I spoke up and said we left tens of millions of francs in Marcel's safe.

When Comrade inquired loudly why no one had told him about Marcel's money, I tried to explain. I told him that originally, we thought Juliette was one of us and considered the money to be hers. And now that Juliette turned out to be self-centered, with no real commitment to either side, the money suddenly sounded like it was for grabs.

Comrade said he did not care about the past, but to try our best to secure every penny, and it could completely finance the revolution in Oran for three months. What was even more important was the fact such finances would help in gathering the scattered freedom fighters.

I also told Comrade the only two people who knew the combination for the safe were Juliette and me.

Chapter 16

Comrade asked that Salwa and I meet with him alone. He told the two of us we might need Juliette's help if we were to avoid being detected by the French. I said I could not handle dealing with Juliette anymore and he needed to find another person or another way. Comrade said we may have no other choice, and our approach should be based on pretending to give the safe money to Juliette for a ten percent cut.

I said if this was the case, then I would not be needed, and instead, any trustworthy person could do the same after I had given him the combination. Comrade was blunt and said, "She may need more than her ninety percent cut."

Salwa and I both knew what he meant. Salwa tried to rush out of the room, but Comrade grabbed her by her arm, stopping her.

She said nothing.

Comrade then said, "If you think I am making this decision lightly or cavalierly, you are mistaken, but if you think I am going to sacrifice human lives for a love affair, you are also mistaken."

This was the first time Comrade mentioned our love affair openly.

Salwa lost her inhibition, grabbed my arm, and said, "I want you to do it. I can handle it."

"I am not a sex machine," I said, "like you and Comrade think of me."

I pulled free of Salwa's grasp, nodded my head quietly, with a sense of forced and sad resignation. Comrade left the room and Salwa tried to soothe my feelings. I was not in the mood to accept her attempts. That evening, I kept to myself, trying to reconcile what I had gotten myself into. I felt I was no longer in control of my own body.

In the morning, Salwa tried again unsuccessfully to cheer me up. I went into a corner and reflected quietly.

She approached me a third time and said, "What do you want me to do? Do you think I am happy about such a prospect? I am being torn into a hundred pieces on the inside, and so scared this bitch will entrap you instead of us entrapping her. Your life will be at stake. Every time we think it is over, things get more demanding and messier. I am going to talk to Comrade and tell him we need time off after this operation. We are human and I think we have reached our limit. I can no longer see you sad and withdrawn. If you can't snap out of it for me, do it for yourself. You deserve to feel accomplished, having come all the way from a life of comfort and luxury, and having lost Suhaila."

I gave Salwa a chagrined look and said, "Let it be. I will take care of it, and if we are successful, I will feel much better. Just give me some time."

Salwa kissed me on the cheek and said, "You should feel better, since Comrade is not asking me instead of you."

I was shocked at her statement. Although it was said in jest, it made me think theoretically speaking it could have been worse, yet I knew nowhere in the Arab world, the culture would ask a female to compromise herself, even for the purpose of supporting the revolution.

———————

Comrade took me to see Juliette that afternoon. She was being well taken care of. I used reverse psychology and pretended I was there to scold her for reporting us to Toulouse and endangering our lives. Her answer was that I betrayed her.

I told her I had not, and it was Salwa who was after me, and since she was originally on her way to France, I thought our relationship was over. I added Salwa was not going to replace her, and I had already bought a ticket back to Amman to get engaged to Suhaila.

She asked as to who Suhaila was, as if she was trying to deny that she'd ever heard of her. I was sure Juliette had not heard of Suhaila's engagement to Musa, so I continued with the story as if Suhaila was very much in the picture. Somehow, Juliette was more comfortable hearing about someone far away, than watching me being kissed by Salwa.

When she asked if we could be together again, I told her I could not have anything romantic with her, and I had already told Salwa the same, ostensibly choosing Suhaila over the two of them. I knew I was violating Comrade's plan to use my contrived relationship to bait and switch Juliette, should Juliette insist on renewing such a relationship. Yet, I felt too used and barren in that respect. I wanted to be free of Juliette's demands, although every time I looked at her, I was looking at a beguiling beauty queen.

When she heard Salwa accepted my plans to go back to Suhaila, she said she would try to accept the same, yet she did not want to cut all relations with me, and she would try having me as a friend. I could barely believe what I was hearing.

"Since you and Salwa have accepted my situation, I want to reconcile the two of you. I want the three of us to become friends."

———————————

That evening, I saw Salwa and told her about Juliette's position.

"Are you sure she means what she says? Or is she playing a game like we are?" she asked.

"I'm ninety-nine percent sure she's genuine," I said.

Comrade sent me a message saying we needed to move within the coming forty-eight hours. I went back to Juliette and told her we intended to set her free, but we planned to send her off to France. I pretended I did not know and asked her if she had clothes for the trip.

She said she didn't. This gave me an opportunity to tell her we would try to help her go to the house and fill up a suitcase of clothes. I continued with my pretense and asked if she was carrying any cash. When she said she was not, I told her then we would get some cash from the safe for her trip and beyond.

After checking with Comrade, I took Salwa with me and made the two reconcile superficially.

We three and three fighters proceeded on horseback to Juliette's house. We watched the house for two hours and when we could detect no movement, we tried to enter from the back. As we entered, it smelled as if someone was cooking.

Cautiously, we went up the stairs to find Michelle preparing food. All eight of us took a sigh of relief. Juliette went to her room to pack. There, she must have made a phone call.

Michelle came to me and said soldiers in an armored vehicle were approaching the house. Juliette then burst out of the room and slapped Michelle hard. It became obvious that Juliette had betrayed us again. Before I could respond to Juliette's betrayal and actions, Michelle took me by the hand to observe another armored vehicle with another three soldiers.

I called on the Algerian fighter with the bazooka and asked him if he could disable one of the two vehicles. He said he would if the French military presence was limited to the two already there. He went down and hid behind a large trunk of a tree, aimed at one of the vehicles, and destroyed it, killing all three soldiers.

Apparently, Juliette had not relayed to Toulouse we had a bazooka. Sadly, the second armored vehicle took aim at the tree and a piece of shrapnel managed to kill our fighter.

We watched the exchange from the second floor of the house, fearful they would blow up the house with their big cannon, and us with it. We didn't fire on the second vehicle because it posed no threat to our car. Salwa identified them as foreign legionnaires: highly trained and vicious mercenaries.

Their number comprised of Frenchmen and others from all over the world, especially from French colonies.

I told Juliette I had planned to help her take as much of the money as possible, but because of her betrayal, she was getting nothing. She spat in my face.

Before I could react, Salwa appeared and slapped Juliette's face hard. She yanked Juliette by the arm and tied her to the huge handle of the safe, after making one of the remaining four fighters hide inside it. When I objected, Salwa said she wanted to use Juliette as a distraction.

Salwa, Michelle, one fighter, and I hid in one room and the other two fighters hid in the opposite room. We had handguns, and the fighters had machine guns. With her cooperation, we tied Michelle up and laid her on the floor, on her back, to show she was French.

As the three soldiers came up to the second floor, they looked around for a while before they located the safe. The three French soldiers were helping Juliette. Salwa asked Michelle to yell for help, as loud as she could. The plan was to separate the three soldiers from each other. Two of them ran toward the voice they had heard.

The Algerian fighters on the opposite side surprised them and killed one of the two before the other fell on the ground and killed one of the fighters and wounded the other. The third French legionnaire proceeded toward Juliette. As he was trying to untie her, the fighter in the room shot him.

I came out of hiding with my handgun, without waiting to ascertain the legionnaire soldier was dead. His gun was lying next to him. He squeezed the trigger without even picking up the machine gun. I was hit in the leg. Salwa got out from behind a concrete column and shot him in the head.

The soldier who had tried to untie Juliette was still alive. He stopped and headed toward us. Our wounded fighter managed to kill him, but not before he was also shot, this time in the arm. The legionnaires were masters of their trade, and they showed it despite the fact they were ambushed.

In the meantime, Salwa attended to my wound. I told her I did not feel it was life-threatening, and I was able to take first aid measures on my own. She refused to leave my side. She and Michelle helped stop the bleeding, and I was able to limp out.

We went back to the safe to untie Juliette and get the only unscathed fighter out. We ended up with two dead fighters, two wounded fighters and an unharmed one. It was time to decide what to do next.

With Juliette still partially tied up and her mouth taped, Salwa and I discussed what to do as we began stuffing the money. We both agreed we either had to kill Juliette or keep her some place where she could not communicate. The remaining fighter, Kareem, got into the conversation. He said there was no way he would risk keeping Juliette alive. Even transporting her was impossible.

I disagreed. I was convinced that there must have been a better way.

After that heated discussion, I was the one who devised the plan. I checked to see if the second French armored vehicle was operational. I told Salwa that we could tie up Juliette and leave her behind; three days later we would relay her whereabouts to Toulouse.

Kareem reminded me Toulouse would be there in less than a day, to check on his mercenaries. Then I said we could keep her in the safe, disable the button to open the safe from the inside, and then provide Toulouse with the combination to the safe three days later. We would promise Juliette to give her five percent of the money, enough to support her for twenty years. Salwa said the revolution was starved for money and would not consider giving Juliette a penny.

I refused to become a cold-blooded executioner.

While I thought Juliette deserved to die, by warfare standards, I did not want such a memory to haunt me for the rest of my life. To reach a compromise, I committed to funding Juliette for three years.

I knew Salwa would have preferred I give that sum to the revolution, too, but she said nothing. I took the sum from the safe, divided the notes in half and told Juliette she would get the other half in one year, if she kept quiet, and we would know if she did not, since she was the only outsider privy to such information. I reimbursed the revolution for the money I had halved.

In the safe, Juliette was provided with food and water, a big bucket with which to clean herself and several pots in which to relieve herself. She was also provided with a mattress and cover, plus five books to read.

We used the armored vehicle to travel for a few kilometers to a barren and uninhabited place, dug a hole and buried the suitcases containing the money. We went another six kilometers and burned the vehicle before we mounted our horses and rode back to our hiding place.

There, we could not celebrate our mission success since we lost two fighters. It took several days before revolutionary normalcy returned, all with the help of Comrade. With Suhaila gone and Juliette ending up an enemy, I had only one pleasant prospect: Salwa.

It was decision time. With the plan of my return to Jordan, the possibility of leaving Salwa behind and ending a physical and cerebral relationship was on the horizon.

I found myself unable to look Salwa in the eye, and she was reticent to impose her clear but undeclared wishes on me. The situation was not easy. Our hiding place was not inspiring. Its small space and limited facilities, plus the idle time on our hands, started eating at me.

Without telling anyone, frustrated and confused, I chose to exit through the dirty tunnel and attempted to roam outside. The city felt abandoned. I could see no living person, though there were two corpses thirty meters away. I decided not to walk toward them and chose to go the opposite way. Soon I was going through alleyways, which seemed to get narrower and narrower.

As I was looking at the ground, paying no attention to my surroundings, a hood covered my head. My hands were jerked behind my back and tied.

I made a growling sound at first and then asked in French, "What is this? Why? Why are you doing this?"

I was dragged by what I felt were four people. One of them seemed heavy and strong. He gripped my neck from the back with one hand and squeezed it whenever I resisted. It was painful and sometimes his tight squeeze obstructed my breathing.

————————

It felt like an eternity, but it probably took only five minutes to drag me inside. Once my hood was off, I saw what looked like a dungeon. I was facing four guys with hoods the like of which I had seen before in the paper, associated with the Ku Klux Klan. The hoods had two holes for their users to see through.

They asked me if I spoke Arabic, and I answered I was an Arab.

"And when did you start working for the occupiers?" one asked.

I was inclined to say I was working for the revolution, but they could have been French agents, for all what I knew.

Instead, I told them I was working for nobody. They asked me to save myself and not to lie. I told them I was not lying. When they asked where I lived, I gave them the district where my apartment was located. I did not want to tell them my exact address, as it was in a very high-end location.

They followed by asking for my exact address and when they heard it, they were very surprised. Two of them went into the corner and whispered to each other.

I did not know what they said, but right after, I was taken into a smaller dungeon, undressed to my underwear, and was tied to a most uncomfortable chair, with one leg just about to break off. I was trying to balance myself all the time, because if I were to fall, I would not have been able to stand up.

Within ten minutes, I wanted to pee and started making noises. One of them came into the small room and threatened to slap me in the face. I kept nodding my head downward, trying to make him understand I wanted to pee.

He figured it out after a while. He put the hood over my head again, pulled me up, and walked me a long distance. There was no bathroom or commode, just a five-meter hole.

He took my hood off, and I had to stand at the edge of the hole to pee.

I thanked my handler, and he looked at me sideways, as if to say, '*Who are you kidding, trying to finesse your way with a thank you?*'

———————————

After two days with the same routine, with none of the four talking to me, one finally came into the room and said, "Are you a Muslim?"

"Yes, I am. Thank God."

The '*Thank God*' addition was usually used by more religious persons, so I said it in case they belonged to a religious party. He then asked me to pray in a loud voice.

I did what they asked for, but I forgot and pronounced the prayer in classical Arabic, while Algerians did it in their dialect.

I could see the surprise on my interrogator.

"You are not Algerian!"

It was too late to claim I was.

I told him I was Palestinian.

He gave me a strange look and bolted out. Two of his friends came into the small dungeon, seeming bewildered but more sympathetic.

Four days into my incarceration, one of them untied my hands, went into the larger dungeon, and came back with my clothes and asked me to put them on. He said, "My name is Yousef and what is your name?"

I told him, and he said, "I lived in Egypt, and I knew some Palestinians there; they don't use Zine. They use Zain. What is your real name?"

I asked him where he lived in Egypt; he said in New Egypt, a well-known district in Cairo. I then asked him the names of the Palestinians he knew. He named three, and I recognized one of them, Nader Saber, my cousin.

When I asked him to describe him, I knew they were probably active in the Algerian war of independence, as my cousin was a leader in the General Union of Palestinian Students, which supported the Algerian revolt wholeheartedly.

I stood up and extended my hand for a handshake and said I am Suhail Saber, the cousin of Nader Saber. He looked at me and said in a relaxed posture, "If Nader is your cousin, what is physically particular to him?"

I told him he was blind in his left eye because of a fight when he was young.

He held my hand in both of his and said, "I ask for your forgiveness. Please forgive me. We thought you were working for the French. You look different, fair, and wearing fancy clothes, excuse my language."

He then asked what I was doing in Algeria; I told him I was in love with an Algerian girl, and I wanted to take her back to Jordan. I was all the time cussing myself for not having been more daring and avant-garde, failing to share with Salwa that

I wanted her to be in my life, all the way to Jordan. If my kidnapping had produced anything positive, it was that I made my decision regarding Salwa. I decided she was my choice as a present companion and future wife.

Chapter 17

Two hours after I disappeared, Salwa informed Comrade. He sounded an alarm which was heard by a dozen cells of the Algerian resistance. They had no idea what could have happened, and after they received the answers from those cells, they concluded I was captured by the French army.

Many suggestions of how to proceed were discarded, one after the other. After my disappearance for two days, Comrade, in desperate thought, said, "Although we have communicated with Toulouse about Juliette being held in the safe, what about if Toulouse forgot to open the safe and free her?"

He added if they could get to Juliette, she could still be convinced to help in freeing me.

Comrade decided to send two people to observe the house. There was no movement, nor any sound coming out of the house for ten hours. At two in the morning, as instructed, the two entered the house and gingerly opened the safe. There was Juliette, in miserable shape. She had scratched herself all over her body. Her hair was wet and sticky as the temperature rose inside the safe and she tried to cool off.

Although she was out of food, she fortunately was not out of water. Juliette must have suffered from a lack of nutrition and salt and could not walk properly.

The two Algerians thought Comrade was correct that Toulouse had forgotten about Juliette. Toulouse always knew about the money, kept by Marcel, as half of it was supposed to be his. When he could not find the money in the safe, he thought Juliette had hidden the money, 'with the help of the Algerians'.

He suspected she then set up a fake safe incarceration, trying to give herself an alibi. Toulouse also accused Juliette of intentionally causing the death of six of his soldiers, all 'to help the rebels.'

He did not want to execute anyone outright, as he had no authority to do as much to a French national. He intentionally kept her in the safe after his soldiers interrogated her, unconvinced of her story. He planned to claim the rebels kept her there and caused her death.

One of the two Algerians had to go and let Comrade know. Comrade asked devastated Salwa if she wanted to accompany him to see Juliette.

At first, she said, "No," because she felt so guilty, with a great sense of deep loss.

Jameela convinced her to accompany Comrade, after she gave her a bath, a massage, and combed and braided her hair.

As things were tense and the French were collecting even innocent Algerians and executing them summarily, Comrade and his party had to tread most cautiously as they were risking sure death. Their salvation was their possession of the five horses that had been confiscated from the French rancher. In their calculations, the French army always considered either vehicles or on-foot travel; they had not factored in the Algerians using horses.

When Comrade and Salwa got there, they were shocked at Juliette's condition. Salwa took care of Juliette right away. She gave her a bath, fixed soup, and fed her. After she changed Juliette into her pajamas, she put her to sleep.

Salwa woke her up at three in the morning, as the team intended to leave Juliette's house two hours before dawn.

Comrade told Juliette he was willing to give her the halved notes right away if she could help in finding me.

Juliette said she would try but could think of only three friends who could help without informing the French authorities.

She woke up all three early in the morning. Only one of them, Denise Le Marque, was daring enough to help. Denise's husband was a deceased and highly decorated general. After she tried with half a dozen sources, she called Juliette back and told her not to repeat what she was about to tell her. The French were not recording any names of the ones executed, but she could tell her that I was not in prison.

When Comrade and Salwa heard the news, Salwa broke down and Comrade hit his forehead with his palm and started reciting a Koranic verse, "Do not consider those who die for the sake of God as deceased, for they are alive in the presence of their Lord."

Comrade began reciting the last rites verse, which caused Salwa to wail. Juliette asked Salwa why she was so upset, since I had supposedly decided to go back to Suhaila.

Salwa held Juliette by her shoulders, tried to shake her and said, "Suhaila is getting married to someone else! He was mine before they killed him."

Juliette paused for a few seconds and grabbed Salwa and held her in her arms, gliding her hand over Salwa's hair. Salwa cried on Juliette's shoulder and for a few seconds closed her eyes and finally dozed off.

Comrade's team left ninety minutes before dawn, but not before they were delayed by giving Juliette the cut of half of the notes they were holding.

Juliette thanked Comrade and said she would do anything in her control to help find me alive or at least find my body. She asked Comrade to tell Salwa she no longer held any grudges against her, and she sincerely hoped I would surface and reconnect with Salwa. Comrade, being the revolutionary he was, told Juliette he might contact her in the future, and he also could be of help to her.

The team got back to their new quarters before dawn. Comrade told Jameela what Juliette had found and asked her to console Salwa. In the meantime, I refused to give Yousef and his friends any names for them to ascertain my allegiance. I suggested that they ask their contacts about Zine the Palestinian. I told them sooner or later some would recognize who I was. Yousef liked the idea but pretended to be non-committal.

They kept trying across the Algerian resistance cells throughout Oran, but there was no recognition of my name by anyone.

It so happened one of those contacted by Yousef started asking about Zine, on his own. This is when another fighter said his brother, who lived in Almería, had mentioned he had met a Palestinian called Zine. That Algerian contacted Yousef to let him know that apparently there was a Palestinian called Zine.

Yousef asked if he could talk to his brother, Sayed. When contacted, Sayed said he only could recall the name and the conversation about the fact in the Middle East they used a different name for couscous, a name he could not recall at the time.

Yousef called Sayed again and asked him to describe Zine. He told Yousef all he could recall was that Zine's hair was straight, and he was relatively fair, and he was tall. Although they were general descriptions, they fit me precisely. Yousef was convinced the Zine in Almería and I were the same person. He called a third time, having suspected Sayed may have been reticent to share all he knew.

Yousef asked Sayed to call him back if he ever remembered anything which related to 'Zine, the Palestinian'.

Sayed grew suspicious of Yousef and decided to contact Zahra, the woman who hosted Zine in Almería. That alarmed Zahra, and as a result, she contacted Salwa to let her know someone was asking about Zine out of Oran.

Salwa immediately told her Zine was most probably dead and the person who was asking for Zine was fishing for information, as they suspected the French had tortured him and he most likely divulged some information about the resistance to them, but not all. Salwa also told Zahra it would be helpful if she told anyone inquiring about Zine that he was dead.

Zahra felt sad and disappointed for she and her husband, Mohammad, really liked me and appreciated my volunteering for Algeria. When Zahra told Sayed I was probably dead and it was alright to let everyone know I was dead, Sayed decided to call Yousef back. He told Yousef Zine was dead, without giving him any details. Yousef realized then that my kidnapping by his cell was a big mistake, which caused some kind of disruption, the nature of which was unknown to Yousef. This is when he came back to me and told me he had been in touch with Almería, and my friends there thought I was dead.

———————————

I still could not divulge things to Yousef, and instead I told him to tell my friends in Almería I was not dead. Yousef liked my idea; he called Sayed and said, "Tell your friends Zine is not dead, and I saw him yesterday. He is just lost."

Sayed told Zahra, and Zahra told Salwa. Salwa did not want to believe it and thought this was a ruse to entrap her cell and possibly others. Yet, she had to tell Comrade. Comrade told her he was ninety percent convinced it was a ruse, but it could have been for real.

When Salwa called Zahra back and asked her if she had the caller's phone number, Zahra secured Sayed's phone number and relayed it to Salwa the same day. Comrade told Salwa the worst thing they could do was to call the number. Salwa had forgotten about the phone technician in Marseille.

The technician was soon assigned to tap the phone being used by Yousef; it was a public phone immediately next to the dungeons. The phone was watched eighteen hours a day by specially assigned Algerian kids. Once they heard a ring, they would use their slings to alert Yousef and his other cell members. The technician in no time gave Comrade the location of the phone.

Comrade sent three people to monitor the use of the phone. Yousef and his team were the only ones using the phone as they put fear in the heart of the neighbors not to use it. The neighbors thought the team was nothing but a drug-smuggling gang, and Yousef and his team favored such a bad reputation. It was much safer than to be known as rebels. Within two weeks, the three dispatched to monitor the phone, plus the technician, managed to list all first names and chart their movements.

Having concluded there were only four of them, Comrade dispatched twelve fighters. They surrounded the dungeons and waited. Once they had two of the four outside the dungeons, they kidnapped them and then attacked the dungeons.

It so happened Yousef and one other were there. There was no fight; it was over in less than two minutes. I realized what was happening as I recognized a couple of the barging fighters. I completely trusted Yousef and his team as genuine Algerian resistance fighters by then, yet our communication was limited due to our secretive and secure cell structures.

As the ones who recognized me approached to hug me, I said in a loud voice, "No, they are with us. Let them go."

The attacking team thought they were drug dealers. Everyone stopped and listened to me. I said under the circumstances they could risk accepting my kidnappers were on the same side, and added, "If they happen not to be, you still have them under your control."

After exchanging the names of some of the fighters they knew in common, they embraced each other, and they embraced me. I told everyone jokingly if Jameela was not available to give me a bath, I wouldn't go back. At any rate, I told them they had to tell Jameela first, for her to keep her silence until I would have taken my bath, and only afterward I would meet the rest of the group. Above all, I was most concerned about Salwa, as I wanted her to meet me after I was all revived.

They accommodated my requests to the last detail. I was escorted for hours to be greeted by Jameela. She could barely keep my secret; she was dying to tell Salwa. After she bathed me and I had a change of clothes, Jameela lined up everyone there, including Salwa and Comrade, for my grand entrance.

When I got out, Salwa looked at me and fainted in a split second. Again, we woke her up; she saw me and fainted all over again.

Jameela and I had really bungled it. In hindsight, someone should have primed Salwa for the occasion. Jameela poured all kinds of herbal drinks into Salwa's mouth, making sure she did not choke. This helped Salwa wake up.

Salwa looked at me as if she did not know what to do. She alternated between crying and frowning before regaining composure. When she finally got over her shock, she smiled broadly and gave me a huge hug and would not let go.

Chapter 18

I wanted to find a secluded spot to be with Salwa, but the place was very small and resembled a tight pedestrian crossing. We were behaving like teenagers, grabbing, and kissing each other whenever we could find a few seconds to be alone. Jameela was aware of and sensitive to our situation.

She could tell how anxious we had become not being able to be alone. She worked hard at it, and in the end, managed to serve the food far from where we were, attracting everyone away from us.

She winked at Salwa, and Salwa took me by the arm into the bathroom. There, she spread two bed covers. We kissed, fondled, and made love, trying not to make any noise.

It was most satisfying: mutual warm feelings and hot desires, all happening now that both Suhaila and Juliette were out of the picture. I told her the one-year deadline related to Suhaila and nobody else, and since Suhaila was out of the picture, I was extending my stay to help my Algerian brothers.

This is when she looked at me and said, "You and others always forget your Algerian sisters."

She was right; the Algerian men and I came from a male-dominated culture, where women played no role in liberation movements. It was not the case in Algeria; they played a major role.

I apologized to her and promised to correct myself in the future.

She said, "You should include your sisters all the time, but do not include me; I am not your sister."

I felt she was indirectly inquiring as to the nature of our relationship to each other.

I said, "No, you are not my sister. You are everything to me, now and in the future."

I could see it in her eyes, inquiring as to what I meant by now and in the future.

I looked at her and said, "Do you think I can imagine a future without you? If you want to, you will be part of me and part of my future."

Her stare said it all; she was craving further elaboration.

I added, "When the time comes, I want you to be my wife, if you accept me as your husband."

She reacted in French, reverting to her youth when she lived in France. "*Mon Dieu, je ne peux pas croire que j'entends ça,*" meaning "My God, I cannot believe I am hearing this."

I told her what I was telling her was my true feelings.

She replied, "I love you, Suhail. I fell in love with you the first moment I saw you."

This was the first time she had used my real name. I guess she felt our expressions were real, prompting her to use a name associated with my reality.

I asked her how she knew my real name.

She said I once addressed myself as Suhail while making love to her.

Our exchanges got more frequent and less challenging as we developed a system of where to hide and when. At one point, I mentioned we needed to talk about Jordan, and for her to meet my father. She immediately asked about my mother.

I told her she would also meet my mother, but my mother opposed anything and anyone I associated with, if it had not been initiated by her. On the other hand, I told her my father was a humble and very successful angel who came from severe poverty to build one of the largest engineering companies in Kuwait.

Salwa said she was looking forward to seeing Jordan and meeting my parents, but before she could do that, she had to see her father. I was surprised, as she never talked positively about him, but rather critically, and with hate and disgust to ward him. I asked if she wanted to see him alone, or with me.

She answered, "No, with you. Your help and presence will be necessary."

I did not think much of her statement, although I was curious as to why my presence would have been helpful.

Days passed by, during which the resistance was reestablishing itself, after so many of its members were killed, executed, and jailed. At a minimum, our movement got easier and more hiding places became available.

The original team—Salwa, Jameela, and the girls—moved to larger quarters. The new place was left by a settler who moved to Spain, leaving the key with a concierge-resistance fighter.

The concierge would call the settler daily to make sure he was not showing up unexpectedly.

Furthermore, Generalissimo Franco introduced strict new measures at the border, which targeted Algerians but hampered the settlers as well. A sudden return of the house owner from Spain was a remote possibility after the measures were put in.

———————————

Salwa and I occupied separate rooms in our new quarters, though they were adjacent to each other, courtesy of Jameela. The house was so lavish, I had to teach everyone how to use some of its gadgets. The most convenient gadget included an elaborate speaker system, whereby one can buzz and talk to thirteen different locations in the house.

Salwa and I used the speaker system to plan our own rendezvous. Finally, I could smell and squeeze her, without anyone threatening our interactions, and with Jameela protecting us. Above all, I thought the house was a prelude to introducing Salwa to luxury living, for my parents' house was larger and fancier than this one.

During such rendezvous, Salwa slowly but surely and systematically introduced her plan to visit her father. I could not understand why it was supposed to be so intricate and elaborate, since it was a family plan. I thought her father's misdeeds may have created a sense of dread; thus, she wanted to be ready for every possible reaction on his part.

It was possible she was afraid he may not receive her with open arms, and he could even receive her in a violent rage, since she had refused to have anything to do with him for a very long time, while he was anxiously looking for her.

Two weeks passed before Salwa told me the plan was in place, ready for my accepting one of the possible dates. I told Salwa I was ready anytime she was, provided she checked with Comrade first. She said she had already told him. Accompanied by another resistance fighter, Salwa and I would take the forty-kilometer trip together. I was surprised when Salwa asked if I could give her a thousand dollars, which I did.

It became apparent after we began our trip that she had a specific use for the money I provided. We took the three horses for fifteen kilometers, where we were met by a taxicab, with a French-looking driver, Jibran, an Arab name.

His original name was Jobert, a French name, which he used until he realized who his mother was and how she died. She was intentionally killed, courtesy of his father, after she gave birth to Jobert.

After Salwa told us about Jibran's background, she admitted she had connected to four Algerians with a similar background as hers, products of settler rape of an Algerian mother. Just like Salwa was, it turned out the driver was biologically half-French. He also was one of the four.

She said Jibran was going to help, and there was another, Hani, meeting us in front of her father's winery house.

"Why all this similar background business?" I could not control myself; I felt I had to ask Salwa about it.

She gave me a most evasive explanation: "What could be better than people working together based on their common experiences, just like you and me?"

"What do you mean by a common experience?"

She said she would explain everything before she got to her father's house.

Before Jibran drove us through side streets and windy alleys, she gave Jibran two hundred dollars. He tried to give it back, but Salwa insisted. In one hour, we got two blocks from her father's house and met Sammy. She gave Sammy another two hundred dollars. His reaction was the same.

She then told me both were in bad need of money as they were suffering from psychological challenges. I suspected the two were hired hands; Salwa assured me they were not.

I asked her to explain what was going on, as I could not connect the dots.

She took me to the side and said, "This is my real revenge day. My real revenge was not against Marcel or Juliette; it is against my father. This is the day I am going to kill him, to avenge the death of the dearest person ever on this earth, my poor mother."

I had totally neglected to consider this scenario and was surprised and bewildered by the whole thing. I had forgotten what she had said months earlier and felt the thought of killing her father had faded away. She had kept it from me and did not divulge it until it was too late to seriously challenge it. I understood that she could not follow through with my plans of being forever together until she accomplished this last daring and emotionally exacting mission.

I paused for a long and most pensive time.

"Will you come back with me and forget about this for your own good?" I asked.

"I want to be with you the rest of my life, but I want to be fulfilled, with all my rage and revenge behind me, too. I have to do this," she said resolutely.

I had to pause again, and then said, "This may bring nightmares in the future, nightmares you cannot see or feel right this minute."

"You don't think I considered that possibility?" she asked. "I did, and I am convinced if I do not do it, I will suffer greater nightmares anything else imaginable could cause. I don't have nightmares often anymore because I have been consumed by my plan to kill him. This preoccupation helped me feel normal. Now, I can no longer pretend the opportunity is not at hand. On the contrary, if I don't go through with it, I will have unbelievable guilt and nightmares, possibly the rest of my life."

This was when I asked her if she would let me kill him instead. She refused.

Salwa had maintained contact with a half-Algerian and half-Spanish housekeeper, Carolina. Carolina facilitated our entry into the house, waiting for Guy Antoine to come back.

Carolina's involvement was easy to secure; she had been raped by Guy Antoine dozens of times. Jibran pretended he was called to Guy Antoine's house for a ride. He kept one of the security guards occupied while Hani distracted the other.

We entered the house with no resistance. Salwa waited in the living room while Sammy and I waited in her father's office.

Guy Antoine came in, not suspecting anything. He called for Carolina.

Salwa stood up from behind a Louis XIV chair, carrying a machine gun and said, "She may have committed suicide, just like my mother did, since you raped Carolina on a regular basis. I am here to kill you, Guy Antoine, because you might as well have killed my mother with your own hands. Your basic and barbaric impulse tortured her for the rest of her life. She loved me so much; she waited until I became an independent adult before she committed suicide, all because of what you did to her."

"You are my daughter. A daughter cannot kill her father, and a father cannot kill his daughter. I know. I know you will not be able to pull the trigger, and besides, look at you. You are the product of what your mother and I had together," Guy Antoine said, trying to change Salwa's mind.

"Had together? I am the product of a violent rape, but I am my mother's daughter, and nothing in me is part of you. I have to kill you because you are evil and a killer, and you are still doing to others what you did to my mother. I know. I saw Marcel's records. You are not only a Black Feet settler; in your chest there is a dark heart which pumps your blood into your veins," said Salwa.

Salwa must have felt a strong lump in her throat, as she bent forward to clear it. Guy Antoine took out a handgun and aimed it at her, but before he pulled the trigger, Carolina appeared out of nowhere, ten meters from Guy Antoine with a shotgun. She pulled the trigger, and I could see Guy Antoine thrown backward, bleeding but not dead.

Guy Antoine turned around, aiming his gun at Carolina. But again, before he could pull the trigger, Carolina took a couple of steps toward him and again fired her weapon, hitting him in the face, pulverizing it into dangling pieces.

I ran into the living room after Guy Antoine fell on what was left of his face. I checked his pulse; there was none. I grabbed a sheet off one of the tables and covered Guy Antoine's face, and ran toward Salwa, grabbed her, and kissed her on her forehead, and walked her away to the office.

I told everyone, including Carolina, we had to leave right away. The two security guards heard the shots and realized they were being misled. One tried to pull his gun and was killed by Jibran. The other surrendered to us.

We got back to our horses where we planned to rest for a while. While Salwa shed no tears witnessing the murder of her father, she was suddenly nauseated and experienced stomach cramps. She was throwing up every few minutes, her face pale and countenance withdrawn. She lay on the ground, and we were unsure whether she was resting or if she had passed out. After we poured water on her face and head to revive her, she was able to partially wake up.

She whispered in my ear that this sort of physical reaction to remorse had happened before. Noticing my skepticism, she explained that vomiting was an involuntary way for her body to expel guilt.

That kind of reaction was new to me, as I had no knowledge of psychosomatic conditions. I gave her a kiss on the cheek and we both left it at that.

She mounted my horse behind me and wrapped her arms around my waist. I was concerned her convulsions could repeat, as the first series was severe and very scary. We got to our luxury house with Salwa in a feeble state. She went to bed right away, attended by Jameela.

———————

We quickly smuggled Carolina into Almería while the other security guard was kept by the resistance for a potential prisoner exchange. The following day, Comrade was incensed at Salwa's misleading presentation. In response, Salwa apologized and told him that psychological wounds were more important than physical wounds, and she had to take care of this one so she could lead a normal life in Jordan. On behalf of us both, she said goodbye.

Comrade knew our relationship might lead to such a plan but did not realize it would happen so suddenly.

He said, "Not so soon; there are things I need to take care of before you leave our ranks."

Both Salwa and I thought he was referring to another mission. Comrade said he would share the details with us the following morning. Our wait was uncomfortable as we did not know anything about what Comrade was talking about.

At six in the morning, Jameela woke the rest of us up, and we were summoned to the living room. At the other end of the room, there was a spread and hung white sheet.

Comrade faced me and Salwa and said, "I have with me a member of the revolutionary council, and he wants to address the two of you."

A figure appeared behind the sheet. The man's features were not definable. He praised our work as heroes of the revolution. He then said we both would receive the highest medals to be bestowed by the free republic of Algeria, after independence. He added he wished he could be closer to give us each a kiss, and to rest assured that just by looking at us, he felt the revolutionary fervor of our work.

"I hope you feel the eternal gratitude of the revolution." He wished us peace, success, and a happy life together, and left. The whole affair took less than seven minutes.

Everyone there kissed Salwa and me, showing the warmest emotions, and expressing all their gratitude.

Neither I nor Salwa knew what to do. Salwa shed tears of thanks and joy, and hugged Jameela so tightly and with sincere affection.

Comrade said conditions were ideal for us to leave for Almería right away, and for us to be ready in one hour. We hurried and packed. Neither of us had many clothes. Before I left, I gave Jameela eleven hundred dollars, to give everyone in the house a hundred dollars each. Jameela thanked me and said Zahra and Mohammad would be giving us items to take with us to Paris.

"Paris?" I asked. "We are not going to Paris. We are going through London."

"No, you are going through Paris. Zahra will explain."

I said nothing.

———————

We left in a hurry. Comrade was right; it was not hard to challenge Franco's strict measures. Salwa and I left for Almería after the most emotional goodbye to the girls, especially to Jameela. At the door, Yousef was there. I had never seen Comrade so emotional.

He hugged me and said, "You have been an inspiration. Go in peace and take care of our princess. She is also a valiant pride of this great and noble revolt."

Chapter 19

When we got out of the boat in Almería, we were met by four men. Seemingly, they had heard about some of my accomplishments, possibly embellished and exaggerated. They were all most welcoming, cheerful, and exceedingly helpful and exhibiting a good mood. They took us to Zahra and Moham-mad's home. There, over forty people cheerfully welcomed us. They were all Algerian supporters of the revolution except for one Spaniard.

He was in his late forties, called Juan. When I inquired about him, I was told he had been once a partner in three wineries, in Algeria, and he found his settler-partner was raping Algerian girls. He sold his shares to his partner and never had anything to do with the settlers ever again. After which, he started sup-porting the Algerian revolution in a big way. His father was a Republican who fought against Franco and was later executed.

Everyone had heard about the FLN bestowing upon us a special medal. It was a great celebration. Zahra had instructed everyone not to ask us anything. It was a little bit strange, as many had difficulty carrying out a conversation with me, trying to obey Zahra's guidelines. They were able to talk comfortably with Salwa as she was much more versed in Algerian social chit chat than I was.

Juan approached me and said, "We have everything ready for you."

I looked at Zahra and she nodded twice, her sign of approving my talking to Juan.

He told me I was scheduled to leave for Madrid, then Paris in three days, and in the meantime, I was staying with him, 150 kilometers from Almería.

I could not help it; I looked at Zahra again. She again nodded her head.

Juan did not speak any Arabic, but he spoke English fluently. After a tumultuous welcome, I had to tell Salwa we were heading out with Juan. She also looked at Zahra and Zahra again nodded, as if she knew I was relaying to Salwa what Juan had told me.

Juan told me to say goodbye to Zahra and Mohammad, as I would not be seeing them before leaving for Madrid. Zahra grabbed my face and kissed me several times and said, "You are one of the honorables."

For a second, I thought she knew my background, but I figured right away she was making a general reference. She grabbed Salwa's face and said, "You have honored us with your presence. Go in peace, and may you live long and happy with your honorable husband."

At the door, I bowed to the gathering and said, "You have honored me by accepting my participation in your struggle, and I can tell you that liberation is nearer than you think. I saw and participated in this glorious struggle, and I know I left back in Algeria thousands of valiant heroes."

Zahra spoke with a loud voice and said, "God will be your guardian and those guarded by God cannot be vanquished."

We left with Juan, riding in the back seat, while a security man sat next to him. Juan explained the father of the security man, Alejandro, was a Republican too, also executed by Franco. He told us he was having a small gathering in our honor; all were sons and daughters of Republicans executed by Franco. They, Juan included, were not being watched and harassed by the Franco regime because they successfully changed their surnames and backgrounds.

After Salwa and I showered and put on fresh clothes, we called on Juan to tell him my clothes were not ironed and Salwa did not have any fancy clothes for the occasion. In no time, Juan had my clothes ironed and provided Salwa with one of his late wife's dresses. When we joined the gathering, we were received so warmly, "as if we were royalty," like they say.

Juan advised the guests not to ask detailed questions. One of the guests, Alfredo, gave me a pen, and he said it was one of his father's pens. He said that based on what he heard about me, I seemed to mirror the struggle his father went through. When I inquired about the similarities between me and his father, he said his late father was a Frenchman who volunteered to help the Republicans, got married to a comrade-in-arms, his mother, the same as I was getting ready to marry Salwa.

When I asked if his mother was alive, Alfredo said she was, and she was spared execution since her father was a Catholic archbishop and Franco did not want to further defy the

Church. He also told me the person who would be taking care of us in Paris was his paternal cousin, Bernard.

I asked him what Bernard did. He said he owned several businesses, and one of them was a winery. I asked him if it was coincidental both Juan and Bernard owned wineries.

Alfredo said it was not; It was part of Juan's reaction to the 'hunt' by the settler wine owners. Juan wanted to create a counter winery association to fight against such rapes and to support progressive movements.

I called on Salwa to join us. Alfredo gave Salwa another of his father's pens. He told me and Salwa that Bernard was taking care of all our expenses in Paris, all through our five-day stay. Neither I nor Salwa knew we were staying five days in Paris. I had been under the impression we were connecting the same day to Amman.

I briefed Salwa about my conversation with Alfredo.

She was excited and anxious to visit where she was mostly raised. This is when she let loose, hugged me, and kissed me all over, not to mention she rubbed from my head all the way down my torso, to my waist. I was pleasantly surprised but tried to change the interaction, as many were looking at us, all admirably. I shared with her that I believed the group was very committed and trustworthy because of their common experiences, a theme Salwa very much believed in.

The gathering was the best Salwa and I ever had. The level of warmth, trust, and commitment was way beyond our expectations. With everyone's statements and expressions, we felt emotionally so connected to the struggle in Algeria, all in a most giving and luxury-abundant atmosphere.

After the gathering, Juan said he intended to go over the plans with us in the morning.

Juan looked at us and said, "I have prepared two adjacent rooms for you two."

When we got to the rooms, we found out they were linked by a common door.

In the morning, we were fitted by two tailors, one for me and another for Salwa, to make two suits for me and three dresses for Salwa. Within nine hours our new clothes were ready, and they fit us reasonably well. Juan checked them out and said they were okay, as far as he was concerned. He asked us what we thought, and we told him they were very fine. Salwa's were almost haute couture.

When she tried her dresses on, she thought they were very fancy and said she needed to get used to wearing fancy clothes of that kind.

No sooner than we tried on our new clothes, Juan knocked on the door and came in. He asked for the already packed clothes and turned them inside out. He showed us that the clothes they prepared for us had very narrow, well-hidden pockets on the inside. We were surprised as we did not know what the purpose of those pockets were. Juan said that the pockets would conceal special fuses.

When I inquired about the fuses, Salwa said, "They are bomb fuses, used to blow up things."

I was well aware of their uses and benefits to the revolution.

When I asked Salwa if she knew in advance, she said "No," but she had handled them in the past blowing up French facilities in Algeria.

Juan gave us two first-class tickets to Paris, London and then to Amman. He told us a two-room suite was reserved for us at the Plaza Athénée. When I asked about the Plaza Athénée, he said it was the best hotel in all of Paris and possibly in the whole world. He added we were reserved for one night in London at the Connaught Hotel, which could be the second-best hotel in the world.

When I said we might not need the reservation at the Connaught since we would have delivered the fuses by then, he said things had to be in line; otherwise, we would raise suspicions if we were to stay at a first-class hotel in one city and at a third-class one in another.

He continued, "And make sure the concierge at the Plaza Athénée is aware you are staying at the Connaught in London. He will automatically vouch for your status."

Over time, I found out that at the beginning, I was green relative to activists in liberation movements, and I was equally green relative to European high society's norms and standards. Salwa seemed to have put away her revolutionary struggles faster than I did. She was just beside herself, enjoying every aspect of our stay in Spain. In her room that abutted mine, she fixed herself coffee and tea three times each and munched on all the goodies left there.

She would walk and then stroll, sometimes straight and sometimes undulating. She would look at herself in her new dresses and sometimes she would take them off and look at herself in her new slips and underwear. I thought she was having a weird reaction to the setting as she was only paying attention to herself, as if I were not there.

After an hour of this behavior, she jumped onto the bed next to me, and said, "Will we live in a house as fancy as this?"

I told her we would be living in two separate apartments, albeit next to each other.

"How about your parents' fancy house?" she asked. I told her the first thing I would do upon arriving in Amman was to arrange leasing two apartments, to keep us separate from my mother.

Salwa said that she could not be that bad, referring to my mother. I told her what my father had told me: that she had severe paranoia, and she could not help the way she behaved.

Before we left Spain, we were so thankful to Juan, as our stay was most comfortable and enjoyable.

At the airport, in Paris, we were screened rather thoroughly. After we answered the most routine questions of name, age, and address, each of us was asked about the hotel we were staying at, and when we said Plaza Athénée, the officer seemed to change his tune.

Within thirty minutes, we were out of customs, to be met by none other than Bernard. After he kissed Salwa and shook hands with me, he led us to his fancy Citroën. He drove us to the hotel and asked the concierge to reserve dinner for four at a very fancy restaurant.

He went up to our suite and asked that we change. He then took Salwa's dress and my slacks and said he would bring them back to us when he was supposed to pick us up for dinner.

After he removed the fuses, he came back to meet us.

On the way to pick up his wife from her legal office, he told us that his wife knew of his political activities but did want to know any details, and asked us to speak mostly in generalities, when it came to politics. We followed his advice, and when his wife asked Salwa as to her favorite clothing designs, Salwa told her in Algeria people did not pay much attention to fashion, all because of the war taking place there. The evening went fine.

Bernard provided us with one of his cars and a driver, and we were taken all over Paris and the surrounding areas. Our tours were all organized, and our restaurant reservations were all taken care of, courtesy of Bernard. The five days went by fast and pleasantly.

After our stay in London, we dressed up for the flight to Amman. We thought we looked very handsome. Salwa had an easy time going through customs as she held a French passport. When my turn came, I was interrogated for over an hour, and then they frisked me all over.

The officer checking my jacket, which I had taken off, felt something solid. He tried to find out what it was, but he could not find it. I offered to help him. I felt the same thing, but I could not figure out how to get to it. After almost twenty minutes, the officer found the item. Seemingly, the guys in Paris failed to remove one of the fuses. I got nervous. I suspected the officer was going to accuse me of preparing to blow up something in Jordan.

He accused me of attempting to smuggle the fuse. His voice and demeanor indicated it was something serious. I did not know what to do, especially when he asked me if I had a receipt for the fuse. When I told him I did not even know a fuse was there, he said, "Who do you think I am, a moron? Of course, you knew where it was, and you were trying to smuggle it in. It must be very expensive."

This is when my father showed up, after he asked for special permission to go into the customs area. He heard part of the conversation and the accusations as he approached. When he asked the officer, he was told I was trying to smuggle a small but very expensive item.

My father took out ten Jordanian dinars and slipped it in the hand of the officer. I was out of customs in a split second. I knew then it was all a shake down for an under-the-table tip, a practice which was officially illegal, but practiced by even the higher ups. My father drove us to our apartments, where we left our bags and proceeded to see my mother.

When my mother saw me, she hugged me and kissed me over twenty times, and at the same time ignored Salwa. My father had to intervene to stop my mother, as she did not know when to stop. Salwa was smiling, more so about my mother calling me Susu than about her being ignored.

In the end, my father could not take it; he had to physically take my mother's arms off me, and he then introduced Salwa.

When Salwa said in Arabic she was honored to meet my mother, my mother said, "Sure you are honored; we are members of the Honorables, which includes my son but not my husband."

My father said to Salwa, "I cannot tell you for sure if they are jack assess or mules. You can take your pick, based on your impressions."

That was the last time I had Salwa accompany me to see my mother. I knew she was too unhinged to be tolerated by new acquaintances. We, her family, considered it our duty to absorb her insults, for the most part. I visited her only when my father made his monthly trip from Kuwait.

———————

Salwa loved Amman because it was peaceful. She was sought after by neighbors and friends alike, and she was so humble and charming. We both enrolled at the university.

One early morning, we ran into Musa. He tried to avoid me. I went after him and said, "You don't need to avoid me. Neither you nor Suhaila meant to hurt me. Things happened the way they did because it was both our kismet. I want you to say hello to Suhaila and to tell her I do not begrudge the fact you are engaged, and I offer you my best wishes. By the way, this is Salwa, my fiancée."

When Musa heard I had a fiancée, he loosened up.

He welcomed her and shook her hand with what looked like sincere congratulations. Salwa told Musa she heard so many good things about Suhaila, and to say hello to her. Musa left saying he would convey our warm regards to Suhaila.

In a few weeks, we ran into Musa and Suhaila. We stopped them and after some chit chat, I asked them when they planned to get married. The wedding was scheduled after the school year. I told them Salwa would love to attend their wedding so that she could compare Palestinian weddings to Algerian ones.

Musa looked at Suhaila and then she said, "Sure, sure, why not? You are most welcome. We will send you an invitation in the mail."

I ran into Musa another time and we had a cup of coffee together. When I asked him where they were having the wedding, he said, "Where else? At the refugee camp."

I grabbed Musa's arm and said, "Look at me, we are both Palestinians, and my family could have ended living in the camp just as easily, the same as yours is doing right now. I know you are proud of yourself and proud you are going to college, just like your brother, who is now an established engineer in Saudi Arabia. I would like to make you an honest offer, and it is up to you to accept or turn it down; just say yes or no. I now think of Suhaila as my sister, and I want the best for her; I am ready to pay for your wedding to Suhaila at the best hotel in Amman. I hope Salwa and I will become friends with you both."

He looked at me and said, "Thank you for your offer. May God increase his bounty to you. I will relay your message to Suhaila and let you know. Again, thank you for your offer."

———————

Two weeks later, we ran into him again. Musa said Suhaila would be proud to accept my offer, and they would like to thank my father and mother for such generosity. I told him my father would be most grateful, but my mother had nothing to do with this offer, and I had not forgiven her for treating Suhaila the way she did. Unless she apologized to Suhaila, Suhaila should have nothing to do with my mother.

"Let bygones be bygones," Musa said.

"Yes," I said. "Bygones can be bygones, after an overdue apology takes place."

Salwa, my father, and I went to Suhaila's and Musa's wedding, and we all enjoyed ourselves a lot, especially Salwa. Dr. Hamadah and I visited at the wedding. He reminded me I had not gone back to see him since my return. He told me if I did not visit him regularly, he could not continue to keep his promise.

I inquired which promise he was referring to. He said it was the promise of keeping my and Salwa's glorious sacrifices to the Algerian revolution secret.

I did not take his statement seriously, except he must have meant what he said. His contacts in Cairo had told him about my experience in Algeria, and he could not hold himself back. When I failed to pay him any visits, he told everyone he knew, among the liberal and progressive segment of the society in Amman, about my supposed heroic adventures with Salwa.

Before long, people began to stop both of us on the street, shaking our hands. It got to a point when we were asked to give speeches about our experience. I convinced Salwa if we were to start, we could not later stop it. Finally, we did start, as keynote speakers when the war in Algeria ended in July of 1962. It was a glorious day, all through the Arab world.

My mother tried to scuttle my plans to marry Salwa, using some of the most devious tactics. She spared no one on her side of the family, using them to put pressure on me to change my mind. She even organized a *Jaha* to go all the way to Algeria, which is usually a family committee to ask for the bride's hand. As expected, Mona never went to the trouble of checking on Salwa's background. Salwa had only distant relatives left.

Instead, this unusual committee was assigned to prevent the marriage from taking place. When I finally convinced her that I was adamant, she tried to take over the arrangements for the wedding, including bathing and dressing the bride.

I could only imagine what my mother could have done after looking at Salwa's two bands of tattoos, one around her breast and another around her crotch. I think she would have spread the news all over the country. Those bands were my emotional and revolutionary pride, for me to add to my respect and love for a valiant rebel with a noble cause.

The wedding took place in 1963 at the plushest hotel in Amman, with the help of our friends and admirers, and it was a grand event. Though things were running smoothly before it began, my father and I could clearly observe my mother's anxious and agitated demeanor. She was about to burst into action.

My father made sure nothing of the sort happened. After he coached me, we cornered my mother in a separate room and I relayed the following, with all intended implications but with the softest of deliveries.

"My father plans to humble you by exposing the true value of your 'Honorable' lineage. He has your back dowry all ready and he will divorce you in public, if he must."

I was trying to shock her into realizing the seriousness of the situation. Both my father and I had reached our limit.

She actually went into shock and started crying.

"You don't need to cry if you behave yourself," my father said. "Pull yourself together and put on a cheerful face. We only have one son, and this may be the most important day of his life. If you truly love him, you will do what I am saying and try to love your daughter-in-law. She is an angelic gift, and she makes him so happy. She should do the same for you."

———————————

I welcomed Salwa, who had chosen a colorful, traditional Qabil Algerian wedding dress. She looked radiant but above all she told me she felt she was walking on air. Everyone admired her. When she arrived to stand by my side, everyone clapped and cheered, and a dozen women ululated loudly.

My mother could not avoid noticing all the cheer and joy around her. She was flanked by eight close friends my father assigned to control any unexpected behavior on her part.

At the wedding, I told Musa and Suhaila I also did not pay a penny since one rich and progressive admirer volunteered and insisted on paying for the whole affair. Musa felt even better than he had before, since the 'affluents', like I was supposed to be, also accepted handouts.

———————————

I had two years left before I graduated with a bachelor's degree in engineering, and Salwa returned to school for her master's in political science. Even after two years, Salwa felt elated at the turn of events.

She savored the transformation into a tranquil and comfortable life. She loved my friends and family and kept her distance from my mother, as per my advice.

She intermingled and adapted without adopting the superficial aspects of Amman's society. To her surprise and mine, she started speaking Arabic with a Palestinian dialect, something neither she nor I expected to happen so soon.

Amman to Salwa was, like the Arabic proverb says, 'a pot that found its lid'.

Acknowledgments

As this is my fifth Palestinian love story, I conclude it with special thanks and acknowledgment to my wife, Eileen, who has been my ardent supporter despite her severe medical challenges.

She faced such challenges with an unbelievable air of optimism, one that has continuously lifted her and my spirit during both good and testing times.

W agih Abu-Rish is a Palestinian American author and activist. His novels are thematic love stories, dealing with social and political issues pertaining to the Arab world. He spent much of his career as a businessperson, specializing in acquisitions. During a long and varied professional career, he was a foreign journalist in Lebanon and an ad executive on Madison Avenue, in New York. Mr. Abu-Rish earned his bachelor's and master's degrees in journalism from the University of Houston and University of Oregon, respectively. This is his fifth novel.

Made in the USA
Middletown, DE
05 December 2025

24170921R00156